THE CASE OF THE BORROWED BRUNETTE
THE CASE OF THE BURIED CLOCK
THE CASE OF THE FOOTLOOSE DOLL
THE CASE OF THE LAZY LOVER
THE CASE OF THE SHOPLIFTER'S SHOE
THE CASE OF THE FABULOUS FAKE
THE CASE OF THE CROOKED CANDLE
THE CASE OF THE HOWLING DOG
THE CASE OF THE FIERY FINGERS
THE CASE OF THE HAUNTED HUSBAND
THE CASE OF THE MYTHICAL MONKEYS
THE CASE OF THE SHAPELY SHADOW
THE CASE OF THE GLAMOROUS GHOST
THE CASE OF THE GRINNING GORILLA
THE CASE OF THE NEGLIGENT NYMPH
THE CASE OF THE PERJURED PARROT
THE CASE OF THE RESTLESS REDHEAD
THE CASE OF THE SUNBATHER'S DIARY
THE CASE OF THE VAGABOND VIRGIN
THE CASE OF THE DEADLY TOY
THE CASE OF THE DUBIOUS BRIDEGROOM
THE CASE OF THE LONELY HEIRESS
THE CASE OF THE EMPTY TIN
THE CASE OF THE GOLDDIGGER'S PURSE
THE CASE OF THE LAME CANARY
THE CASE OF THE BLACK-EYED BLOND
THE CASE OF THE CARETAKER'S CAT
THE CASE OF THE GILDED LILY
THE CASE OF THE ROLLING BONES
THE CASE OF THE SILENT PARTNER
THE CASE OF THE VELVET CLAWS
THE CASE OF THE BAITED HOOK
THE CASE OF THE COUNTERFEIT EYE
THE CASE OF THE PHANTOM FORTUNE
THE CASE OF THE WORRIED WAITRESS
THE CASE OF THE CALENDAR GIRL
THE CASE OF THE TERRIFIED TYPIST
THE CASE OF THE CAUTIOUS COQUETTE
THE CASE OF THE SPURIOUS SPINSTER
THE CASE OF THE DUPLICATE DAUGHTER
THE CASE OF THE STUTTERING BISHOP
THE CASE OF THE ICE COLD HANDS
THE CASE OF THE MISCHIEVOUS DOLL
THE CASE OF THE DARING DECOY
THE CASE OF THE STEPDAUGHTER'S SECRET
THE CASE OF THE CURIOUS BRIDE
THE CASE OF THE CARELESS KITTEN
THE CASE OF THE LUCKY LOSER

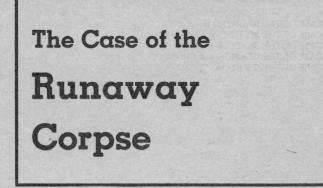

The Case of the
Runaway
Corpse

Erle Stanley Gardner

BALLANTINE BOOKS • NEW YORK

Foreword

Few people have any idea of the duties, the responsibilities and the uncanny detective skill of an expert medical examiner.

Some time ago, in Los Angeles County, a six-year-old girl was murdered by a sex maniac. It was the sort of crime that aroused a surge of indignation, followed by a wave of fear.

The sex killer was still at large. No one knew who he was. The murder had been unbelievably vicious and depraved, and startled parents everywhere realized that no child was safe until the killer could be apprehended.

The battered, mutilated body was brought into the coroner's office, where Dr. Frederick D. Newbarr went to work.

The police had searched for weapons. They had found an ax and a knife.

Dr. Newbarr examined the body, with its multiple wounds, then said to the police, "Go back and search until you have found an ice pick and a ball-peen hammer. It is my opinion that those weapons were also used."

Then Dr. Newbarr did something no autopsy surgeon likes to do but which occasionally he is required to do under circumstances of stress and emergency. He dissected the tissue around the wounds and by a process of pathological deduction determined the sequence in which the wounds had been administered. Taking the four weapons in order, he determined which weapon had been used first, which second, which third and which fourth.

The police did splendid work in that case, but that work was sparked by the painstaking efforts of Dr. Newbarr. And when the killer was finally apprehended he made a detailed confession. That confession showed that the crime had been committed and that the weapon sequence was exactly as Dr. Newbarr had deduced in his laboratory.

Incidentally, we hear a great deal about crimes the police fail to solve. But how many times do we stop to think back and, as citizens, give thankful credit to cases of this sort where intensive, shrewd investigation runs down a sexual psychopath who is completely unable to control the distorted urges of his perverted emotions? Such a man will live quietly and unostentatiously, well known in his neighborhood as a mild-mannered, inoffensive neighbor, until some time when his surging emotions will take charge of him, independent of his own will, and transform him into a veritable maniac.

Dr. Frederick Newbarr is more than an expert pathologist, coroner's physician and autopsy surgeon. He is a medical detective.

He has done a great deal of work in the field of distinctive pattern wounds, and has, so far as is known, been the first to employ some techniques in the field of criminal investigation which have heretofore been used only in England and in Europe.

Dr. Newbarr spent many long hours working on the baffling mystery of the famous Black Dahlia case.

Since the police have not as yet closed their books on that case, and never will close them until the killer is apprehended, there are certain things which cannot be disclosed at this time.

But there is one interesting incident which indicates the thoroughness with which Dr. Newbarr works, and shows the peculiar problems a medical examiner is apt to encounter.

In the stomach of the Black Dahlia, Dr. Newbarr found certain peculiar threadlike particles which he simply couldn't account for. Apparently they were very small particles of wax which had entered the girl's stomach some time before her death.

This was such an unusual finding that Dr. Newbarr spent hours trying to find some reason that would account for the presence of wax in the girl's stomach.

Finally he solved the problem. The Black Dahlia had very bad teeth, and, according to her associates, when she was going out on a "heavy date" she would rub wax over her teeth so as to conceal some of the unsightly blemishes and cavities.

So this poor girl, thrilled at the prospect of a "heavy date," had carefully waxed her teeth that night in order to make herself more attractive to a man who not only murdered her, but who perpetrated such a series of diabolical and revolting mutilations on the body that even hardened police officers became sickened at the sight.

One needs only to work on the investigation of some cases where an inept autopsy has been performed in order to appreciate the work that is being done by men like Dr. Newbarr—men who are highly specialized in a field which, for want of a better name, I refer to as criminal pathology.

A list of Dr. Newbarr's activities indicates something of his background:

Clinical professor; head of the Department of Forensic Medicine at University of Southern California; guest lecturer at the College of the Medical Evangelists; Chairman of the Southwest Regional Committee of the Educational Committee of the American Academy of Forensic Sciences; member of the Sub-committee on Education of the Committee on Medicolegal Problems of the American Medical Association; and Chief Autopsy Surgeon of the Coroner's Department of Los Angeles County.

Dr. Newbarr is a patient individual who starts on the trail of a criminal with dogged determination. There is a quiet, deadly persistence about him.

One of the best criteria to determine the efficiency of a medical examiner is reflected in the attitude of the criminal attorneys who specialize in defense work.

These attorneys are among the shrewdest practitioners at the bar. They learn to take a man's measure rapidly and accurately, and if there is any weak point in his investigative reasoning or his characteristic reactions, they can bring out such weaknesses on cross-examination so as to cause a maximum of discomfiture to the unhappy witness.

On the other hand when an expert is well grounded in his field, and absolutely certain of the position he has taken because he has carefully thought out all of the factual ramifications, defense attorneys leave him strictly alone.

Dr. Newbarr is very seldom subjected to any extensive cross-examination these days. For the past few years attorneys have made it a point to ask him one or two routine questions and then quit.

I asked Dr. Newbarr about this and asked him how he accounted for it.

Dr. Newbarr's answer was indicative of the man.

"If any cross-examining attorney can embarrass you on the witness stand it's your own fault," he said. "He's dealing with you in your own field. If you aren't sufficiently familiar with it so that an attorney can embarrass you, it means that you've been careless in your work. A man should never be careless in work involving life or liberties."

Dr. Newbarr could carry that statement just a little further. Dr. Newbarr isn't careless in anything—period.

Among the men who are broadening the field of forensic medicine so that it is becoming of ever-increasing significance, Dr. Frederick D. Newbarr is recognized everywhere as an important leader.

And so it gives me great pleasure to dedicate this book to my friend:

DR. FREDERICK D. NEWBARR

—Erle Stanley Gardner

Cast of Characters

Chapter 1

Della Street, Perry Mason's confidential secretary, entered the lawyer's private office and said, "There are two women in the outer office who say they have to see you at once."

"What about, Della?"

"They won't discuss it with a mere secretary."

"Then simply say that I can't see them."

"They're quite a team," the secretary said.

"In what way?"

"They're carrying suitcases, keep looking at their watches, apparently are catching a train or a plane and feel they simply *must* see you before they leave."

"What do they look like?" Mason asked, his curiosity aroused.

"Mrs. Davenport is very, very mousy, a quiet, almost furtive, plain young woman."

"How old?"

"Somewhere in the late twenties."

"And very mousy?"

Della Street nodded.

"And the other?" Mason asked.

"If I describe Mrs. Davenport as being very, very mousy I'll have to describe Mrs. Ansel as being very, very catty."

"How old?"

"Fifty odd."

"Mother and daughter?"

"Could be."

Mason said, "The dear, devoted daughter has had to put up with too much from a brute of a husband. The daughter's mother has come down to remonstrate and the husband called her a lot of vile names. She and her daughter are leaving him forever. They want their rights protected."

"Probably," Della said, "but they're quite a team, anyway."

"Tell them I don't take domestic relations cases," Mason said, "and that they'd better hurry to see some other lawyer before their plane leaves."

Della Street seemed reluctant.

Mason picked up several letters from the file marked "Urgent" which Della Street had placed on his desk. "You want me to see them," he charged, "so that you can gratify your feminine curiosity. On your way, young woman."

Della Street dutifully left the office, only to return within some thirty seconds.

"Well?" Mason asked.

"I told them," she said, "that you didn't take cases involving domestic relations."

"And what did they say?"

"The mousy one said nothing."

"And the catty one?" Mason asked.

"The catty one said that this was a murder case and she understood you *liked* murder cases."

"And they're still waiting?" Mason asked.

"That's right. The catty one suggested I tell you they had a plane to catch."

"That does it," Mason said. "Send in the cat and the mouse with their murder case. My own curiosity has now been aroused."

Della Street hurried from the office, returned in a few moments to hold the door open. Mason heard the sound of steps, of a suitcase bumping against a bookcase. Then a slender, demure-looking woman with downcast eyes entered the office carrying a suitcase. She looked up briefly, said, "Good morning," then moved quietly along the wall and was lowering herself into a straight-backed chair when another suitcase banged vigorously against the door. An older woman pushed her way into the office, dropped the suitcase with a bang, looked at her wrist watch and said, "We have exactly twenty minutes, Mr. Mason."

"Very well," Mason said, smiling. "Please be seated. I take it you're Mrs. Ansel."

"That's right."

"And this is Mrs. Davenport?" Mason asked, indicating the young woman who sat with her hands folded on her lap.

"That's right," Sara Ansel said.

"Your daughter I take it."

"No, indeed," Sara Ansel said. "We never even saw each other until a few months ago. She's been out of the country a lot—her husband's a mining man—and I've been in the Orient, in Hong Kong. I'm sort of her aunt by marriage. My sister's husband was her uncle."

"My mistake," Mason told her. "Do I understand that you want to see me about a murder case?"

"That's right."

Mason studied the two women thoughtfully.

"Did you ever hear the name of William C. Delano?" Mrs. Ansel asked.

"Wasn't he a big mining man?"

"That's right."

"He died, I believe."

"Six months ago. Well, my sister's husband, John Delano, was his brother. John and my sister are both dead now. And Myrna here, that is Mrs. Ed Davenport, is a niece of John and William Delano."

"I see. Now suppose you tell me what it's all about and about the murder."

"Myrna's husband, Ed Davenport, has written a letter accusing Myrna of planning to kill him."

"And to whom did he send the letter?"

"He hasn't sent it to anyone yet. He left it addressed to the district attorney or the police, we don't know which, and it was to be delivered in the event of his death. It accuses his wife of poisoning Hortense Paxton, the niece who would have inherited the bulk of William's money, and then Ed Davenport has the temerity, the unmitigated gall to state that Myrna suspects he knows what she's done and may be planning to poison him, that in the event of his death he wants the whole thing investigated."

Mason glanced curiously at Mrs. Davenport, who sat perfectly still. Once, as though sensing his gaze, she raised her

3

eyes, then lowered the lids again and continued to regard her gloved hands.

"What in the world," Mason asked, "gave him any such idea as that? Does he have any grounds for such accusations, Mrs. Davenport?"

"Of course not!" Sara Ansel said.

Mason continued to look at Mrs. Davenport.

She said, "I spend most of my time in my garden. I have some sprays, some pest controls. They're highly poisonous. My husband has a besetting curiosity. Twice now I've had to warn him those sprays are not to be tampered with. That may have given him ideas. He's very unreasonable. He gets ideas and they become fixed in his mind."

"He's neurotic," Sara Ansel explained. "He broods. He drinks. He flies into rages, and then he gets strange ideas."

"Apparently," Mason said, "there's rather a complicated picture here. I'll have to know something more about it, and I take it you're leaving on a plane."

"That's right. We have a taxicab waiting. The driver has given us a deadline. We're going to have to make the airport in time for the 11:00 A.M. plane to Fresno."

"Perhaps," Mason said, "under the circumstances it would be better if you took a later plane and—"

"We can't. Ed's dying."

"You mean Ed Davenport, this young woman's husband?"

"That's right."

"And he's left this letter to be delivered to the authorities in the event of his death?"

"That's right."

"That," Mason said, "complicates the situation."

"Doesn't it?" Sara Ansel said impatiently.

"What is he dying from?" Mason asked.

"Dissipation!" Sara Ansel snapped.

"Perhaps," Mason went on, "it would be better if you tried to give me a more complete outline of the background."

Sara Ansel settled herself in the client's big, overstuffed

chair, giving a series of wiggling motions that expressed aggression rather than relaxation.

"Now you'll have to listen carefully," she warned, "because I'm not going to have time to repeat."

Mason nodded. "My secretary, Miss Street, is taking notes. I can study those later."

"William C. Delano was a very rich man and a very lonely man. During the past two years of his life his niece, Hortie—that's Hortense Paxton—came to live with him. He was dying by inches and he knew it. His will left most everything to Hortie. She was nursing him. It was a terrific job. She wrote Myrna and Myrna and Ed came to help with the nursing.

"After they'd been there a short time Hortie became very ill. She died after a week's sickness. Ed Davenport didn't say anything at the time. Later on he told Myrna he thought Hortie had been poisoned. Where he got that idea no one knows. It's typical of Ed Davenport—a neurotic, addlepated mass of selfish pigheadedness."

"What was the cause of death?" Mason asked.

"Overwork. Her death was a terrible blow to William. She was his favorite niece. Under his will he had planned to leave her four-fifths of his estate and one-fifth to Myrna."

"He left you nothing, Mrs. Ansel?"

"Eventually he did. He and I never got along too well. After Hortie died he changed his will."

"You seem positive Miss Paxton's death was a natural death."

"Of course it was. She had this intestinal flu that's going around. Only Hortie was so run-down she couldn't fight it off."

"Did you see her before her death?"

"Yes. I came there when I heard she was sick to see if I could help. I got there three or four days before she died, but I didn't stay long after that.

"William Delano and I were fond of each other but he irritated me to death and I guess I clashed with him. Myrna insisted she could get along all right, what with the housekeeper and a practical nurse they called in, so I left."

"And when did you return?"

"Shortly after William's death."

"Was there any autopsy at the time of Miss Paxton's death?"

"Of course not. There was an attending physician and he signed the death certificate. She was buried and that was all there was to it until Ed Davenport started this talk of his. If you ask me the man simply isn't all there. What's more he's trying to divert attention from what he's done with Myrna's money.

"Ed has these crazy ideas, and now he's gone so far as to write that letter to be opened in the event of his death. The fool has high blood pressure. He may go any minute, and yet he's written this dastardly letter. In the event of his death there's no telling what may happen."

"Where is that letter?"

"Up in his office somewhere."

"Where's the office?"

"In Paradise."

"How's that?"

"That's the name of a place up near Chico in the northern part of the state. His office is in a house there. It's the house where he and Myrna lived for a while after they came back from South America. Ed got hold of this mine on a shoestring deal. After he and Myrna came down to Los Angeles to live with William, Ed fixed the house up in Paradise as an office for his mining company.

"That is, he says it's an office. Two rooms are fixed up as offices, but he has a bedroom and a kitchen. He spends a lot of time up there. He'll be gone for a week at a time, sometimes two weeks. Since I've been with Myrna he's spent most of his time up in that place he calls his office—and in gallivanting around the country, playing he's an economic big shot, the great mining magnate."

"May I ask," Mason inquired, "how it happens that you are so intimate a part of the picture—that is, I take it there was no love lost between you and William Delano. You—"

"After all, I'm fond of Myrna. Under the new will, I own a one-fifth interest in that big house of William's. I'm not going to let Ed Davenport put me out of my own house. After

I saw how he was treating Myrna I became terribly indignant, but I've tried to keep my place and not say anything. I haven't, have I, Myrna?

"Then we got this telephone call this morning that Ed is in Crampton and—"

Mason said, "I gather he had been taken ill?"

"That's what I've been trying to tell you—he's dying and we only have a few minutes left. The very idea of any man writing a fool letter like that to be delivered to the authorities in the event of his death, accusing his own wife of murder."

"Is that what's in the letter?"

"As nearly as we can tell, putting two and two together, that's what's in the letter."

"And how do you know what's in the letter, Mrs. Davenport?" Mason asked.

Myrna said in a voice that was so low it was difficult to understand her, "He said as much. He got mad and accused me of poisoning Hortie and said since I knew he knew what I'd done, he didn't feel safe himself."

"And Mr. Davenport is in Crampton now?" Mason asked.

"That's right. He started down here from Paradise and got sick. He's in a motel. The doctor is quite alarmed about him—thinks he won't live."

"And if he does live?" Mason asked.

Sara Ansel said, "Well, of course, *I'm* not one to give advice. Myrna can do just as she wants, but as far as *I'm* concerned Ed Davenport has been juggling her money, mixing it all up with his. I'm absolutely certain he's going to try to cheat her out of it. I know what *I'd* do if I were in Myrna's place."

"And if Ed Davenport dies?" Mason asked.

Sara Ansel looked across at Myrna Davenport.

"If he dies," Myrna Davenport said in her soft, almost inaudible voice, "that letter will be delivered to the district attorney and heaven knows what will happen."

"And what do you want *me* to do?" Mason asked.

"Get the letter," Sara Ansel snapped.

Mason smiled and shook his head. "I'm afraid I can't help you there."

"I don't see why not."

"I can't steal that letter."

"It contains slanderous matter," Sara Ansel said.

"Nevertheless," Mason said, "the letter is his property during his lifetime."

"How about after his death?"

"Undoubtedly he left instructions for it to be mailed to the police."

"As it happens," Sara Ansel said, "all of the property that he has is community property. It was all acquired with Myrna's money, regardless of the fact that Ed Davenport has been busily engaged trying to juggle funds around so that no one can tell where the money came from."

Mason's face showed interest.

"Now then, suppose he *does* die. Myrna, as the widow, is entitled to step into possession of the property. Isn't that right?"

"For the purposes of administration and to conserve it for the administrator," Mason said guardedly.

"Then she's entitled to the possession of that letter."

"Go on," Mason said, smiling.

"I don't think it's fair for that letter to fall into the hands of the police and the district attorney without Myrna knowing what's in it."

"Of course," Mason said, "a great deal depends on how the letter was written, or, rather, I should say, how the envelope is addressed—whether it's addressed to the police to be opened in the event of his death, or whether it's addressed to his secretary with instructions to her to mail the enclosure to the district attorney in the event of his death."

"That would make a difference legally?" Sara asked.

"It might," Mason said. "I'm not in a position to render an offhand opinion."

Abruptly Sara Ansel got up from the chair. "Give me your key, Myrna."

Wordlessly, Myrna opened her gloved hand, handed Sara Ansel a key. She, in turn, walked across and dropped it on the plate glass on Mason's desk.

"What's that?" Mason asked.

"The key to the office in Paradise."

"And what do you want me to do with it?"

"In case Ed Davenport should die, we want you to get that letter."

"Is there any element of truth in Ed Davenport's accusations?"

"Don't be silly! Myrna wouldn't hurt a fly. She came there to help Hortie. Those two girls slaved their fingers to the bone. Hortie's death was brought about purely and simply by overwork."

"And Mr. Delano?"

"He had been dying for months. His heart was shot. The doctors gave him six months to live and he lived twelve. He'd have lived longer than that if it hadn't been for Hortie's death. That broke him all up."

"Then why not let the letter be delivered?" Mason asked. "If his charges are so absurd on their face why not simply explain to the police?"

The women exchanged glances, a brief flicker of an expressive signal that Mason was unable to interpret.

"Well?" he asked.

"It happens," Sara Ansel said, "that the situation isn't that simple. There are complicating factors."

"In what way?" Mason asked.

"Someone telephoned the coroner. It was one of those anonymous calls. This person suggested the coroner had better check the death of Hortense Paxton.

"Of course it was just some busybody, unless it was Ed Davenport himself, but it may make trouble."

Mason thought that over. "Myrna is Ed Davenport's wife," he said. "In case he should accuse her of poisoning Miss Paxton he might be jeopardizing the money his wife inherited—and which I understand he's using. Have you thought of that?"

"We have. Ed hasn't. He doesn't think. He reacts. There's no logic in what he does. Why would he write such a fool letter as that, particularly when he knows he may pop off any minute?"

Mason said, "He must be a psychopathic personality."

"He's a nut. You can't tell what he'll do. He may kill us both. If he had any idea we were here talking with you he certainly would."

Mason reached an abrupt decision. "I'm going with you this far," he said. "If Ed Davenport should die I'll try to find out what's in the letter. If, in my opinion, the letter is the work of a psychopath I'll look into the case, and if everything seems to be in order I'll surrender the letter to Mrs. Davenport. If, on the other hand, there is anything at all that's suspicious about the case I'll turn that letter over to the police, but I'll try and do it under such circumstances that everyone gets a fair break."

"If you only knew Ed Davenport," Sara Ansel said. "He's selfish, neurotic, completely engrossed in his own affairs, his own symptoms, his own feelings, and yet with it all he's shrewd."

"*You* haven't known Mr. Davenport very long," Mason pointed out.

"Well, I've known him long enough," she snapped. "I've talked with Myrna, and I wasn't born yesterday, Mr. Mason."

Mason thought the matter over, then abruptly said to Della Street, "Della, dictate a letter which Myrna Davenport is to sign, giving me complete authority to represent her in connection with any matters pertaining to her domestic relations or her property rights and to take such action as I may see fit in connection with safeguarding these property rights. In the event her husband should die—and you'd better mention in the letter that it's understood he is seriously ill at the moment—I'm to represent Mrs. Davenport in connection with the estate and all matters in connection with the estate. I am to act in her name and on her behalf in taking possession of any property of any sort, nature or description, and do whatever I think may be for her best interests."

Mason glanced at Myrna Davenport. "You're willing to sign such a letter?"

It was Sara Ansel who answered, "You bet she'll sign it."

Mason, however, continued to look at Myrna Davenport. At length she met Mason's eyes and said in a low voice,

"Of course, Mr. Mason. My husband no longer loves me. He's interested in my money, and he's stealing that. Right now and as of this very moment he's trying to scramble my property so completely we'll never be able to straighten things out."

Sara Ansel looked at her watch. "Well, what are we waiting for?" she demanded.

Perry Mason nodded to Della Street.

Chapter 2

Shortly after three o'clock that afternoon Mason's switchboard operator rang Della Street to announce that long-distance from Crampton was calling Mr. Mason, insisting that it was on a matter of the *greatest* importance.

Mason nodded to Della Street. "I'll take it, Della, but you'd better listen in on the call."

Mason picked up his phone and when he had been connected through the switchboard heard the voice of Sara Ansel, urgent and impatient, arguing with the operator.

"This is Mr. Mason, Mrs. Ansel," Mason cut in.

"Well, it's about time!" she said. "Here we are in a jam and your operator has been fiddling around—"

"Well, I'm on the line now," Mason interposed. "What seems to be the trouble?"

"He's dead."

"Davenport?"

"Yes."

There was a moment of silence.

"And," Sara Ansel went on, "Myrna is in complete charge. He left a will leaving everything to her—certainly the least he could have done under the circumstances."

"When did he die?" Mason asked.

"About fifteen minutes ago. It's taken me all that time getting you on the telephone. That operator of yours—"

"Yes, yes," Mason said. "Now the letter that you had reference to—"

"The address in Paradise is on Crestview Drive. You can get there by taking the Southwest Airways which goes to Chico. Rent a car at Chico and it's only twelve miles over good, paved road. You won't have much trouble finding the place but it's a lot better if you don't ask questions. So here's the way you get there. Take the main street through town, then turn left on Oliver Road. At the foot of the grade make a sharp left turn onto Valley View for a very short distance, then turn left again onto Crestview Drive, and it's the last place on the right-hand side.''

"There's no one in the house?" Mason asked.

"There's no one there. The secretary will be off duty. You'll find that—I'm sorry, there's no opportunity to talk any more. Good-by.'' She slammed up the telephone.

Mason hung up the telephone at his end of the line, glanced across at Della Street.

"Do you go to Paradise?" Della Street asked.

Mason nodded.

"And when you get there what do you do?"

"Represent Mrs. Ed Davenport's best interests."

"By finding that envelope?"

"Perhaps."

"And then doing what?"

"That," Mason said, "depends on what we find when we get the envelope. Find out about plane reservations, Della.''

Ten minutes later Della Street reported that by taking a direct plane to San Francisco it would be possible to pick up a Southwest Airways plane that would arrive at Chico at seven-fifty.

"Get two reservations, Della," Mason said, "and let's get started.''

"Two?" she asked.

He nodded. "Don't think I'm going to walk into this without a witness.''

Chapter 3

The DC-3 puddle-jumped the bumpy air after it left Marysville, skimming over small communities marked by clustered lights, over the dark spaces of fertile rice fields, past the glow that marked the location of Oroville, then swept low over Chico and into the landing field.

A taxicab took Mason and Della Street up to the center of town where Mason was successful in renting an automobile on a mileage basis. They found the road to Paradise and started climbing up the long grade.

Light from a three-quarter moon showed them something of the country, brought a startled gasp from Della at the sheer beauty of the scenery as the road skirted the edge of a lava cap and they looked down into the depths of a canyon, where crags of lava threw inky black shadows.

Mason glided past the group of stores which marked the center of the community, found the road where he turned left, and had no difficulty in locating the sharp curve which was the signal for another left-hand turn.

On each side of the road were modern, livable houses, among tall pines, bordered with green lawns. Up at this elevation all of the smoke and smog of the lower valley had vanished and, despite the moonlight, the brighter stars shone with steady splendor.

Della Street took a deep breath. "Just notice the air, Chief," she said. "Pure and pine-scented, clear as crystal. And aren't those beautiful homesites?"

Mason nodded.

"Do you suppose Ed Davenport's place is like these?"

"We'll know in a minute," Mason told her, turning the wheel to the left.

They came to the end of pavement, crunched along on a

graveled road past a neat house with a green fence, and then, as the road ended, turned right on the graveled driveway which swept them through a grove of pines, past thick manzanita, a few apple and pear trees, and brought them abruptly to the porch of a house which, despite the darkness within, seemed somehow to have a friendly, homey atmosphere.

Mason switched off the lights, turned off the ignition, walked around the car, and followed Della Street up on the porch.

"Suppose we'd better ring the bell just in case?" Della asked.

Mason nodded.

Della Street's gloved thumb pressed against the bell button. Musical chimes sounded from the interior of the house.

"Ring once more," Mason said after an interval, "and then we'll try the key."

Della Street rang the second time. After some ten seconds Mason inserted the key in the lock. The bolt clicked smoothly back. Mason turned the knob and the door swung open.

"Now what?" Della Street asked. "Do we use a flashlight or—?"

"We turn on lights," Mason told her. "Using a flashlight would indicate a surreptitious visit. A surreptitious visit would indicate a consciousness of guilt. After all, Della, we've drawn cards in a game where we know very little about the other players and I'm darned if I know what the limit is."

"But we're playing for high stakes?" Della Street asked.

"Definitely," Mason said, groping for a light switch.

The reception hallway flooded into brilliance, showing a hat rack made of deer horns and manzanita. A Navajo rug and two rustic chairs gave the place an atmosphere of sturdy simplicity. A big, oval, antique mirror hung on the wall. The aroma of good, strong tobacco clung to the place as though someone who lived there spent much time smoking a pipe.

Mason went through the door to the left, and switched on lights in a big living room. Della Street followed him through the house, taking one room at a time, switching on the lights until the long, rambling, one-story building had been fully illuminated.

"Now what?" Della asked.

"Ostensibly," Mason said, "we're simply taking charge on behalf of Mrs. Davenport. Actually we're looking for a letter which may have been concealed somewhere in the premises. The question is where?"

"It seems such a silly thing to do," Della Street said.

"What?"

"Write a letter to be delivered to the authorities in the event of his death and then leave that letter just hanging around anyplace without making some arrangements for its delivery."

Mason nodded.

Della Street said, "He *must* have made some arrangements for the delivery of that letter."

"Exactly," Mason told her, "which is why we're going to start our search with the secretarial desk in this office."

"I still don't get it," Della Street said.

"We're following the wishes, in fact, the instructions of our client," Mason told her, "and at least we're finding out what it's all about."

Mason slid back the drawers in the steel desk, disclosing stationery of various sorts, carbon paper, and in a bottom drawer of the desk a whole thick file of correspondence in a jacket marked "For Filing."

Mason glanced at the dates on some of the letters, said, "Ed Davenport's secretary seems to feel that there's no hurry about keeping up the files."

"Perhaps she was waiting for enough correspondence to accumulate to make filing worthwhile."

Mason tried the right side of the desk and found that all of the drawers were locked.

"Got a nail file, Della?"

"Are you going to try and pick that lock?"

Mason nodded.

"Chief, do we have the right to look in there?"

"Why not?" Mason asked. "We're searching for papers for the surviving widow."

"It seems sort of—well, we're intruding upon someone's privacy."

Mason took the nail file Della Street gave him and worked away at the lock. After a few moments a bolt clicked back and the drawers on the right side of the desk came open.

"Those are personal things," Della Street said sharply.

"I know," Mason said, "but we're looking specifically for— What's this?"

"That," Della Street said, "very definitely is a lockbox."

Mason shook the lockbox. "There seems to be just one document in it," he said. "This may be what we want. Despite the look on your face, Della, my curiosity is rapidly overcoming my scruples. I don't suppose you would have such an article as a hairpin on you."

She shook her head.

Mason tried the end of the nail file on the lock. "I'm going to need something smaller than this nail file. A little piece of stiff wire would do it."

"Where," Della Street asked, "did you learn that technique?"

"A client taught it to me," Mason said, grinning. "My only fee for defending him on a burglary charge."

"I suppose you got him acquitted."

"He was innocent."

"Yes, I suppose so. He learned that lock-picking in a correspondence school I take it."

"Strangely enough," Mason said, "he really *was* innocent. The lock-picking was a carry-over from his lurid past. Ah, here's a paper clip made of good, stiff wire. Now it only remains to bend the wire, so . . . to insert it in the back, rotate it slightly, and— Ah, here we are, Della."

Mason opened the lid of the box and took out a fat manila envelope. On the back of the envelope, scrawled in a firm handwriting, had been written, "To be opened in the event of my death and the contents delivered to the authorities," and underneath the writing was the signature "Ed Davenport."

"Now, Mr. Attorney," Della Street said, "perhaps you can tell me the technical rules of law. Is this the property of the widow, does it belong to the authorities, or is it the property of the secretary in whose desk it was located?"

"We'll find out what's in it," Mason said, "and then we'll be able to answer some of your questions."

"It might be better to answer them first."

Mason smilingly shook his head. "We have to know the contents before we can determine our responsibilities, Della."

Mason went to the kitchen, filled a teakettle with water, switched on the electricity in the stove.

"You certainly are making yourself right at home," Della Street said.

Mason grinned. "The story is that a watched pot never boils. Perhaps we'd better look around some more in the office."

Mason led the way back into the office, prowled through Ed Davenport's desk, looked through the files, reading letters, opening drawers.

"Are you looking for something specific?" Della Street asked.

"I'm trying to get the people pictured in my mind," Mason said. "Davenport evidently has a great deal of confidence in his secretary. Apparently she makes out and signs the checks. There's a balance of one thousand, two hundred and ninety-one dollars in the bank here in Paradise. There's some correspondence in relation to mining matters. It is interesting to note that whereas certain letters are addressed to Mrs. Edward Davenport there are answers from Mr. Davenport stating definitely what his wife will and will not do."

"Then—"

"Apparently he didn't consult her," Mason went on. "Carbon copies of replies show that several times letters went out on the same date they were received."

"Perhaps he kept in touch with her by long-distance telephone."

"The bill for last month for the entire telephone service was only twenty-three dollars and ninety-five cents," Mason said, "including the federal tax."

"And all this time," Della Street said, "he had a fear that his wife might be planning to kill him—and then he had to go and die a natural death."

Mason raised his eyebrows.

"Why do you do that?" she asked. "You don't . . . Chief, you don't suppose that . . . that it wasn't a natural death?"

"Why not?" Mason asked.

"But, good heavens! Why . . . then what are *we* doing *here*?"

"We're protecting Mrs. Davenport's best interests," Mason said, "but there are certain things which we can't do. We can't suppress evidence or tamper with evidence, but we really can't tell whether it's evidence until after we get a look at it, can we, Della? Come on, I think that pot is boiling now."

Mason returned to the kitchen. Very carefully he steamed open the sealed envelope, reached inside, took out the papers and unfolded them.

Della Street's sharp gasp sounded above the singing of the teakettle as the water continued to boil.

"Well, there we are," Mason said cheerfully. "Six sheets of perfectly blank paper."

Della Street's domestic tendencies came to the front. With her eyes still on the blank pages she turned off the burner under the teakettle.

"Now what in the world?" she asked, and then, after a moment, added, "Do you suppose there's any secret writing on them?"

Mason moved the teakettle to one side, held one of the sheets of paper over the still-glowing burner on the stove, heated it thoroughly, then tilted the sheet first one way and then the other so that the light would fall on it from every angle.

"Of course," he said, "there *could* be some secret writing which could be developed only by iodine fumes, but—well, we don't dare to assume that there is, and yet it may be dangerous to assume that there isn't."

"Why in the world would a man go to all the trouble of leaving an envelope with instructions that it should be opened in the event of his death and then have nothing in it but blank sheets of paper?"

"That," Mason said dryly, "may be something to which we'll have to find an answer."

"How do you mean?"

"Was there a tube of mucilage there in the office, Della?"

She nodded.

"Well," Mason said, "we'll seal this envelope and I think under the circumstances it may be a good idea if I am careful not to leave fingerprints."

Mason dried off the flap of the envelope over the warm burner of the stove, went back to the office, carefully sealed the envelope, put it back in the lockbox, dropped the lockbox into the drawer, and, by using Della Street's nail file, again locked the drawers on the right-hand side of the secretarial desk.

"Chief, you seem to have some idea," Della Street said, "that . . ." She hesitated.

"That things have been just a little too opportune?" Mason asked.

"Well, yes, in a way."

"They have been very opportune," Mason said. "Ed Davenport died and—"

A woman's voice said sharply, "What are you doing here? Who are you?"

Mason turned.

The tall, rather good-looking young woman who stood in the doorway abruptly whirled without waiting for an answer. Mason heard the sound of running steps, then from the living room the whirring of the dial on a telephone.

Mason grinned at Della Street, walked across to the desk, and picked up the receiver from the telephone.

He could hear the woman's voice on the extension telephone saying, "Operator, get me the police at once. There's an emergency. I'm Mabel Norge, at the Davenport house on Crestview Drive. Someone is in the house ransacking the place. Send police at once."

Mason dropped the receiver back into place. He heard the front door slam.

Della Street raised her eyebrows. "Police?" she asked.

Mason nodded.

"How long will it take them to get here?"

"That depends," Mason said. "Probably not very long."

"Do we try to get out?"

"Oh certainly not. We stay and talk with them."

Mason settled himself in the chair behind Ed Davenport's desk, lit a cigarette.

"Chief," Della Street said nervously, "there's no reason why we couldn't get out the back way."

"Our rented car's out front," Mason said. "The young woman undoubtedly has the license number by this time. It was because of the car standing there and the lights being on that she made such a quiet entrance. She must have tiptoed softly down the passageway. Incidentally I heard her give her name over the phone. It's Mabel Norge. She's Davenport's secretary.

"Definitely, Della, we remain here, and we remain in possession. We have no choice in the matter. When you stop to think of it, we've left rather a broad back trail. Flight would, of course, indicate a consciousness of guilt."

"Nevertheless there's something about this whole thing I don't like," Della Street said.

"So far," Mason said, "we've done everything that was expected of us. Now let's try to be a little more independent."

"What do you mean? Do you . . . ?"

They heard the sound of a siren growing louder.

"That," Mason said, "will be the police. That's good service. Keep very quiet, Della, because they may be a little nervous, perhaps a little quick on the trigger."

They heard the front door again, the sound of voices, then heavy feet. A man with a shield on the lapel of his coat, a gun in his hand, thrust a cautious head into the room, said, "Get 'em up."

Mason tilted back in the swivel chair at the desk, took the cigarette from his mouth, blew a stream of smoke into the air and said, "Good evening, Officer. Come in and sit down."

The officer remained in the doorway, the gun in his hand. "Who are you," he asked, "and what are you doing here?"

"I'm Perry Mason, an attorney," Mason said. "Permit me to introduce my secretary, Miss Street. I am at the moment engaged in taking charge of things on behalf of the widow of Edward Davenport."

The girl screamed, "He's dead? He's dead?"

Mason nodded.

"Then he was murdered!" she said.

"Tut-tut!" Mason admonished. "You're doubtless unstrung but you shouldn't make such wild assertions."

"You're representing Mrs. Davenport?" the officer asked.

"That's right."

"Got any authority?"

"She gave me the key to the place," Mason said, "and a letter of authorization."

Mason casually produced the letter, handed it to the officer.

The officer looked at the girl. "Do you know these people, Miss Norge?"

She shook her head.

Mason said, "I take it you're Mr. Davenport's secretary, the one whose initials on the letters are M.N."

"I'm Mabel Norge," she said. "I'm Mr. Davenport's secretary, and in case he's dead I . . . I have something to deliver to the officer."

"Indeed," Mason said.

"Mr. Davenport had anticipated this situation," she said.

"What situation?"

"His murder."

"Murder!" Mason said.

"Exactly," she snapped. "I have something to deliver to this officer which will prove it."

"Go ahead and deliver it then," Mason said.

She walked over to the secretarial desk.

"Here, wait a minute," Mason interposed. "What are you doing there?"

"Getting the thing that I want to deliver to the officer."

Mason smiled and shook his head. "No, no," he said chidingly.

"What do you mean?"

"You mustn't touch anything belonging to the estate."

"You've been in here touching things."

"Why not?" Mason asked. "*I* represent the wife. She's the owner of one-half the property absolutely. The other half will come to her by right of succession."

"Why, you . . . you . . ."

"Take it easy," Mason said.

The officer holstered his gun. "Now let's get this straight. What's the idea anyway?"

Mabel Norge said, "She killed him. He knew that she was going to try to and he left an envelope giving evidence that could be used against her."

"What do you mean, he left it?" Mason asked.

"He gave it to me."

"And told you to keep it?"

"Told me that in the event of his death he wanted me to open the letter and see that the information was delivered to the officers."

"Did you open it before his death?"

"Certainly not."

"You don't know what's in it then?"

"Well . . . well, only what he told me."

"Did he tell you what was in it?"

"He told me that—well, he said enough so that I knew he was anticipating he might die at any time."

"Certainly," Mason said. "The man was suffering from high blood pressure, arteriosclerosis, and I believe there was a renal involvement. His doctors had told him he might go at any time. I think it's only natural for a man to prepare—"

"But it wasn't that kind of a letter. I mean that wasn't what he had in mind."

"How do you know?"

"From what he said."

"What did he say?"

"He told me that in the event of his death I was to open that envelope and see that the officers got the papers, but that if anyone tried to get that letter during his lifetime I was to destroy it."

"In other words he retained control over the letter?"

"During his lifetime, yes."

"And if he had wanted you to deliver the letter to him at any time you'd have done so?"

"Why certainly. It was his letter."

"Where is it?" Mason asked.

She started to tell him, then thought better of it and said, "I'll get it when I need it."

Mason yawned. "I dare say you will," he said. "Well, Officer, let's close up here and, under the circumstances, in view of the fact that Miss Norge says there's a letter here which may contain something in the nature of an accusation I take it it would be well to see that no one removes anything from the premises."

"We'll remove that letter," Mabel Norge said determinedly. "I'm going to open it right now and give the contents to the officer."

"Oh no you're not," Mason said, smiling.

"What do you mean?"

"Your employment has terminated as of the date of Mr. Davenport's death. You were his agent, his employee, his personal representative. His death terminates your employment, subject, of course, to your right to compensation. But you have no right to touch anything here."

The officer said, "Now wait a minute. I don't know law but I don't want to have any evidence disappear."

"Certainly not," Mason said. "I would suggest that you lock all the doors, and since Miss Norge quite evidently has a key—"

"How did you get in?" she asked.

"I told you I have a key," Mason said. "I have Mrs. Davenport's key."

"She wouldn't have given you a key. I know she wouldn't."

Mason smiled. "In that case, Officer, Mrs. Davenport wouldn't have given me a key, because this girl says she wouldn't. Therefore I couldn't have used that key to get in. Hence I'm not here. Disregard me."

The officer said, "If there's a letter that he left to be opened in the event of his death, a letter that gives any clues as to how he died, we'd better get that letter and put it in the hands of the D.A.''

"The point," Mason said, "is that no one knows that this letter contains any accusation against any person or would give any clue. That envelope may contain a will for all anybody knows."

"Well, let's have a look at it," the officer said. "You're representing the wife. The secretary is here. I'm representing the law. We'll have a look at it."

"No one is going to open that letter until the wife says so," Mason said.

"Now wait a minute. You're being hard to get along with," the officer told him.

"Not as long as you do things according to law. What's your name?"

"I'm Sidney Boom, an officer out of the sheriff's office. This territory is unincorporated. It's county territory."

"That's fine," Mason said. "Now do you want to do things according to law or don't you?"

"Certainly I want to do them according to law."

"All right," Mason said. "As far as the personal property in here is concerned it's community property and the surviving widow has a one-half interest in it and always did have. It's hers. The other half will come to her through probate administration. Technically she has the title to it right now, but the title can't be validated until after the estate has been through probate and the debts paid."

"Well, I don't know the law," Boom said, "but I want to get this thing straight. If there's any evidence here I don't want anything to happen to it."

"That's exactly the point," Mason said. "On the other hand if it isn't evidence but if it is some valuable property I want to make certain that it doesn't leave the estate."

"What do you mean?"

Mason said, "How do I know that this envelope which is to be opened in the event of his death isn't a will? Or perhaps it may be some negotiable securities that he wanted to give to this secretary. For all we know it may be cash."

"Well, the best way to find out what it is is to open the letter and find out."

"On the other hand," Mason said, "it may be something that is of vital importance to the estate, something that should be kept confidential."

"But he gave the letter to his secretary."

"That's exactly it," Mason said. "He didn't. He let her *keep* the letter. He didn't *give* it to her. She has admitted herself that at any time he called for it she'd have given it to him."

"Well, that isn't what I meant," Mabel Norge said. "I meant that he'd given it to me to give to the officers at the time of his death."

"Did he say give it to the officers?" Mason asked.

"It was to be opened in the event of his death."

"He didn't say give it to the officers?"

"Well—I don't remember exactly what he did say."

"There you are," Mason said.

"She's taking notes," Mabel Norge said, pointing to Della Street. "She's taking down everything we say."

"Any objection?" Mason asked.

"Well, I don't think that's fair."

"Why? Did you want to change some of the things you're saying now after you've had a chance to think them over?"

"I think you're horrid."

"Lots of people think so," Mason said.

The officer said doggedly, "That isn't getting past this question of evidence. Now I don't know what's going on here but this young woman who works here says that there's an envelope to be opened in the event of his death, and that there's information in it that may lead to . . . to—"

"To apprehending the person guilty of his murder," Mabel Norge said firmly.

"Are you now stating he was murdered?" Mason asked.

"He may have been."

"But you don't know that he was."

"I know that he expected he might be."

"You also knew that he was under treatment from a physician, didn't you?"

"Well, yes."

"And that he had been advised that with his blood pressure and the condition of his arteries he might pop off at any time?"

"He didn't confide in me in all of his personal matters."

"He confided in you about his wife."

"Well—not exactly."

"Then you don't know what's in that letter except by inference?"

"Well, I know what I thought was in it. We can soon enough find out."

Boom said, "Where is the letter?"

"In my desk, in a lockbox."

"Get it," Boom said.

"Now wait a minute," Mason said. "This procedure is highly irregular and highly illegal."

"I'm taking a chance on it," the officer said. "I'm going to see that this young woman doesn't take anything out of the desk except that letter, but if there's a letter there I want to make mighty certain that nothing happens to it. I don't know who you are but apparently you're representing the widow. You got on the job mighty fast."

"And probably a good thing I did," Mason said, smiling affably. "I'm trying to conserve the estate."

"What do you mean by that?"

Mason nodded toward Mabel Norge, who was unlocking the right side of the desk. "What was *she* doing here at this time of night?"

"She works here."

"At night?" Mason asked.

The officer frowned. "Say," he said, "what *were* you doing here?"

"I—I was driving by and I saw lights," she said.

"Where were you driving to?" Mason asked.

"Just by."

"This is a dead-end road," Mason pointed out.

"Well, I—all right, I drove by. I—"

"Were you coming in?" Mason asked.

"That's none of your business," she blazed.

"There you are," Mason said. "She was here. She had no business being here. She doesn't have any work to do at this hour. What was she doing?"

"Now look," the officer said, "this thing is all mixed up. I don't want to get in bad."

"You're getting in bad right now. The minute you use your authority to touch any article in this room you're in bad."

The officer moved over to stand by Mabel Norge. "I don't want you to touch anything except that one letter," he said. "Now where is it?"

"In a lockbox in this drawer."

"All right. Now I'll take the letter out."

"The box is locked," she said, opening the drawer.

Boom picked up the box, said, "It isn't locked."

"Well—I thought it was. It should have been."

Boom opened the box, looked at the envelope.

"I advise you not to touch that envelope," Mason said.

Boom regarded the envelope in the box, then slowly closed the lid.

"What do you think should be done with it?"

"Turn it in to court as part of the estate."

"Suppose something should happen to it?"

"See that it doesn't."

"You mean I'm to—?"

"Exactly," Mason interposed. "Lock it up. Take it to court. Have the judge of the probate court open it in the presence of inheritance tax appraisers."

Mabel Norge stamped her foot. Tears of exasperation were in her eyes. "Open it, you fool!"

Mason held the officer's eyes with his. "Suppose it's filled with money, perhaps thousand-dollar bills that he wanted to give to his secretary in the event of his death? Do you want to be responsible for tearing open the envelope, asking a probate court and an inheritance tax appraiser to take your word for the amount of money there? Suppose they claim you took out a couple of thousand-dollar bills?

"You know what the law is on a safe-deposit box. You wouldn't dare to open that. Neither would the bank dare to open it. It has to be sealed until it's opened in the presence of an inheritance tax appraiser."

"That's right," Boom said, turning to Mabel Norge

"You fool!" she blazed.

Boom's face turned red.

"I tell you," Mabel Norge charged, "that his wife was planning to kill him. He knew it. There's evidence in there that will connect her with one other murder."

Mason shrugged his shoulders and said, "It's your responsibility, Officer. I take it you're under bond."

The officer hesitated.

"Go ahead and open it," Mabel Norge said. "Can't you see he's just talking, trying to keep you from getting the very evidence Mr. Davenport wanted you to have."

The officer picked up the envelope.

"Wait a minute," Mason said. "Don't take your legal advice from me. Don't take it from that girl. You have a district attorney here. Call him up. Ask him what to do."

"Now there's an idea," Boom said.

He moved over to the telephone.

Mason said, "It is my suggestion that this envelope can be opened only when an inheritance tax appraiser is present. I also suggest that if there is any doubt on your part as to what may happen, that the contents of this evidence be impounded."

"What do you mean, impounded?"

"It's in a lockbox," Mason said. "Take it and put it in a safe-deposit box. But you want to be very, very careful to see that no one tampers with the contents of that envelope."

"Don't let him talk you out of doing your duty," Mabel Norge said. "Open it. Get the evidence."

Mason yawned. "Really this is rather tiresome. I don't like to wrangle. As far as I'm concerned I'm perfectly willing to let you take the envelope in to the district attorney, provided proper precautions are taken to see that the envelope isn't opened by any unauthorized person."

"Well, let me talk with the district attorney," Boom said.

He picked up the telephone, placed the call, then said to the district attorney, "This is Officer Boom. I'm out at Paradise. I'm sorry to bother you at this time of night, but I'm up against a question. I'm dealing with a lawyer here who says he's representing an estate—Ed Davenport died. There's a letter in his office that's to be opened in the event of his death. This lawyer who is representing the widow says no one has authority to open it except in the presence of an inheritance tax appraiser. . . . No, it isn't addressed to the officers. It simply says on the envelope, 'To be opened in the event of my death and contents delivered to the authorities.' "

Mabel Norge said, "Tell him that he gave it to me, that it was in my possession."

"It wasn't in your possession," Mason said. "It was in your desk. Your employment has been terminated."

"Oh, *will* you be quiet! I hate you!" she flared.

"You probably would," Mason told her.

"And tell the district attorney that this woman here is taking down everything that's said," Mabel Norge said.

"Hush," Boom told her. "Let me listen."

Boom listened at the telephone for a while, then said, "This lawyer is Perry Mason. . . . Oh, you have heard of him? . . . Well, the name's rather familiar. . . . That's right. . . . He says he has no objection to the envelope being kept in a lockbox and kept in your custody until it's opened in the presence of the court and an appraiser. He thinks there's money in it. . . . Okay."

Boom hung up.

Mason said, "We are, of course, going to hold you personally and officially responsible, Mr. Boom."

"That's right. I'm responsible."

"You'll take that box in to the district attorney."

"I'll see that it gets to the district attorney."

"You're taking it in at once?"

"Not at once. I've got a job to do out here. I'll take it in to him tomorrow. He said tomorrow would be all right. But I'll take care of it and see that nothing happens to it in the meantime."

"That's fine," Mason said. "I object to your taking it, but

if you insist upon taking it I shall expect you to see that the envelope is unopened."

"Well, I'll take it with me," Boom said. "Now in order to get this thing straight I want to have one of your cards, and in case it should turn out that you're not representing the widow— Well, you're a lawyer. I don't need to tell you your business."

"That's right, you don't," Mason said cheerfully. "Here's one of my cards."

Officer Boom, with the lockbox under his arm, started back toward his car.

"I'm going with you," Mabel Norge said.

Della Street waited until the front door had banged shut, then she looked up at Mason.

"Get that teakettle off the stove quick," Mason said. "Incidentally you might run a rag over it to make sure there aren't any fingerprints, and also polish off the controls on the stove. They may think of that before they've gone very far."

Della Street dashed into the kitchen. A few moments later she was back. "Everything's okay," she said.

"All right," Mason told her, "we'll turn out the lights and let it go at that."

"Chief, that secretary is going to talk Boom into opening that letter."

"Not right away," Mason said. "Our main problem, Della, is to keep that letter intact until after the mucilage has had a chance to dry thoroughly. If they get to fooling around with it too soon they'll realize that the envelope has been steamed open and sealed shut again."

"Well, she's going to talk him into opening it."

"Not until after he's gone to the district attorney."

"You want to bet?" Della Street asked.

Abruptly the telephone bell shattered the silence.

Mason glanced across at Della Street.

The phone rang again.

"Do we answer it?" Della Street asked.

Mason nodded. "You take it, Della. Be noncommittal. Find out who is talking before you say anything."

Della Street picked up the telephone, said, "Hello."

She was silent for a moment, then said, "Yes," and, putting her hand over the mouthpiece, said to Perry Mason, "Bakersfield is calling from a pay station. They're dropping coins."

"Any name?" Mason asked.

"Just Bakersfield, calling station-to-station."

Abruptly Della Street took her hand from the mouthpiece, said, "Hello."

For a moment she seemed puzzled, then grabbed her pencil and made swift notations on a sheet of paper.

She glanced at Perry Mason, her eyes puzzled. "Hello," she said. "Hello . . . hello . . . hello. . . . Operator, my party seems to have been disconnected. I was talking with Bakersfield. . . . You're certain . . . ?"

Della Street gently replaced the receiver.

"What was it?" Mason asked.

"As soon as I said hello a man's voice came on the line," she said. "It was a station-to-station call from a pay telephone booth in Bakersfield. The man said, 'Pacific Palisades Motor Court, San Bernardino, unit thirteen' and then the connection broke. I thought we'd been disconnected. The operator says he hung up."

"Now what the devil!" Mason said. "He didn't give any name?"

"No, it was just a man's voice."

"And on a station-to-station call."

"That's right."

Mason got up from his chair and started pacing the floor. Della Street watched him anxiously.

"What will happen if and when Mabel Norge gets Boom to open that envelope?" she asked.

"Then," Mason told her, "there's going to be hell to pay. Whenever that envelope is opened the assumption will be that I took out the pages which contained evidence, statements relating suspicions, conclusions and accusations, destroyed them and substituted pages of blank paper."

"Can anyone tell that the envelope was steamed open?" she asked.

"Sure. An analysis of the adhesive on the flap will show

that it came from this mucilage container and was not the prepared substance that is used on the flap of an envelope to be moistened and sealed.''

''And then what will happen?''

''Once the accusation is made,'' Mason said, ''we'll find ourselves in a county where we have no friends, where we are looked upon with suspicion and where the authorities may well take action predicated on suspicion.''

She smiled. ''Which is a roundabout way of saying we may be arrested?''

''I may be.''

''Then wouldn't it be advisable to . . . ?''

Again the phone rang.

Mason nodded to Della Street.

She picked up the receiver, said, ''Hello. . . . Yes. . . .'' She covered the mouthpiece with her hand and said, ''Can you take a call from Fresno, Chief?''

''Find out who's talking.''

''Who's calling?'' Della Street asked.

She looked up. ''Mrs. Davenport.''

Mason nodded and Della Street handed him the receiver.

''Hello,'' Mason said.

''Is this Mr. Perry Mason, the attorney?''

''That's right.''

''Just a moment. Mrs. Davenport is calling.''

A moment later Mason heard the flat, toneless monotone of Myrna Davenport's voice.

''Mr. Mason, there's been a terrible mistake. He's gone.''

''Who's gone?''

''My husband.''

''That's what Sara Ansel told me. He died this afternoon and—wait a minute, is that what you meant?''

''No. I mean he's gone. He's *really* gone.''

''You mean he isn't dead?''

''Yes, Mr. Mason, that's what I mean. He isn't dead. He wasn't dead at all. He couldn't have been. He's gone.''

''Where?'' Mason asked.

''I don't know.''

''When did he go?''

"I don't even know that. He got in a car and disappeared."

Mason, fighting back anger, said. "What kind of a run-around is this? What are you trying to put over? Sara Ansel told me distinctly that Ed Davenport was dead. That was around three o'clock this afternoon. She said he had died about fifteen minutes earlier."

"That's what we thought. That's what the doctor told us. We all thought he'd passed away, but evidently he was only unconscious. We didn't know where to catch you before you got to this number and by that time we were pretty much confused because—"

"Where are you now?"

"We're at a drugstore, but we're leaving right away. We'll go back to Los Angeles."

Mason said, "Don't go back to Los Angeles. Catch the first available plane, train or bus for San Francisco, whichever is the first available means of transportation. Go to the San Francisco Airport. Go to the mezzanine floor. Sit there and wait. Now do you understand those instructions?"

"Yes."

"Will you do that?"

"I'll have to ask Aunt Sara."

"Where is she?"

"She's right here."

"Well, ask her," Mason said impatiently.

He held the phone for a moment, conscious of Della Street's anxious eyes, then heard Myrna Davenport's voice, "Very well. We'll follow your instructions."

"Don't talk to anyone. If anyone should ask you questions, don't answer. That relates to *anyone*. Do you understand? Anyone."

"I understand what you're telling me but I don't understand why."

"Never mind understanding why. Do what I tell you," Mason said.

Mason hung up the phone.

He strode angrily toward the light switch.

"What is it?" Della Street asked anxiously.

"Apparently," Mason said, "we have been made the victim of a beautiful double cross."

"And Ed Davenport isn't dead?" she asked.

"According to the latest report he is very much alive and has disappeared—perhaps he's on his way up here or he may have been the man who telephoned from Bakersfield leaving the cryptic message."

"So what is your legal position now?"

"That of having assumed charge of an estate before there was any estate, of having rifled a 'dead' man's effects while the man was still alive."

Della Street thought that over for a moment, then moved into the kitchen, making certain that things were replaced as they had found them, polishing off fingerprints and turning off lights.

Mason met her at the front door. "Let's go, Della."

"Where?"

"Back to Chico, where we turn in this car and catch the first available means of transportation out. We stop over long enough to ring up the Drake Detective Agency and tell Paul Drake to have two operatives cover the Pacific Palisades Motor Court at San Bernardino, to keep an eye on unit thirteen, to report to him as soon as the unit is occupied, by whom, and then keep the place covered. We also have Paul check on Ed Davenport. Come on Della, let's go."

Chapter 4

It was two forty-five in the morning when Perry Mason and Della Street walked into the San Francisco Airport.

"You go up first," Mason said, indicating the mezzanine. "Look around. If they're up there beckon to me. If anyone seems to be shadowing them, don't beckon but come downstairs and report. Just take a good look around."

"How can I tell if anyone is shadowing them?"

"If someone is sitting up there reading a paper or a magazine, apparently completely engrossed in something else, let me know. Let's not walk into any traps."

Della Street climbed the stairs, and after a few moments came down to say, "There's a man sitting there reading a paper, Chief."

"And the two women are up there?"

"They're up there, apparently sound asleep. Both of them with their heads back and their eyes closed."

Mason said, "Della, there's a three-five plane to Los Angeles. Get four tickets. We can just about make it. I'll go up and get the women. If they're being shadowed we can't help it."

Mason climbed the stairs. The man who was engrossed in the newspaper casually turned a page, folded it and went on with his reading.

Mason walked partway around the mezzanine, came back, stretched, yawned, settled himself down beside Sara Ansel, who was gently snoring. Myrna Davenport's head was resting against Sara Ansel's shoulder. She was sleeping peacefully.

Mason touched Sara Ansel's arm.

She fidgeted uneasily.

Mason looked over at the man who was reading the newspaper, then touched her again.

Sara Ansel wakened with a start.

"I beg your pardon," Mason said casually, putting a cigarette in his mouth. "Do you have a match?"

She started to glower, then recognized him and said, "Why, I . . . I—"

"And may I offer *you* a cigarette?" Mason asked.

The man with the paper still seemed completely engrossed in his reading.

Myrna Davenport was awakened by the voices.

"Why, how do you do?" she said. "I—"

Mason frowned her into silence. "Do one of you ladies have a match?"

Myrna Davenport produced a lighter.

Mason lit his cigarette. "Thank you very much," he said. He stretched, yawned, settled back in the chair and said in a low voice to Sara Ansel, "There's a three-five plane for Los Angeles. Della Street, my secretary, is getting tickets. She'll meet you at the gate with tickets and gate passes. She'll hand them to you unobtrusively. Get on that plane. We'll talk there."

Mason again yawned, looked at his watch, walked over to the balcony, looked down and received a signal from Della Street that the tickets were all okay.

The lawyer walked casually around to the far side of the balcony, again looked at his wrist watch, settled down in a chair, leaned back and smoked contemplatively while he watched Sara Ansel and Myrna Davenport descend the stairs.

The man who had been reading the newspaper got up, walked to the railing around the mezzanine and casually raised his right hand. Then he returned to his chair.

Mason arose, walked across to the stairs and went down to the main floor, moving slowly, yet timing himself carefully. He reached the gate where the three-five plane was loading two minutes before the time of departure.

Della Street was waiting with a plane ticket and gate pass.

"The two women aboard?" Mason asked.

She nodded.

"Let's go," Mason told her.

They boarded the plane and were able to secure seats directly behind Sara Ansel and Myrna Davenport.

Sara Ansel turned to say something to Mason but he almost imperceptibly shook his head and settled back against the seat.

They fastened safety belts. The motors throbbed into life and the big plane taxied slowly down the long runway, wheeled into position and waited while the motors were gunned into life one at a time. Then the four motors simultaneously roared into a cadence of power. The big plane swept down the runway and into the air. A few moments later the lights of San Francisco showed beneath as the plane made a long, banking circle, then swung out on its course.

Sara Ansel turned and said angrily, "It certainly took you long enough to get there!"

"Up in that country," Mason told her, "they roll up the sidewalks at nine o'clock. We had quite a time."

"What's the idea? Having us running around like a couple of criminals."

"You have your suitcases?"

"No."

"Where are they?"

"We shipped them by air express. We didn't know what you wanted."

"That's fine," Mason said. "If you aren't encumbered with baggage you can move around a lot more easily. Now tell me what happened. We'd better change seats. Della, you sit over with Mrs. Davenport. Mrs. Ansel, you come back here with me."

They changed seats without seeming to attract attention from any of the other passengers, most of whom had settled back, trying to get some sleep.

"Put your mouth close to my ear," Mason said. "Talk low and tell me what happened."

"Do you want the highlights," she asked, "or—?"

"Give me the highlights first," Mason said, "then I'll ask questions to get the details I want."

"Well," she said, "it seems that Ed Davenport left his office in Paradise Sunday noon. He telephoned Myrna that he was driving down, that he would stop overnight along the road.

"He probably stayed that night at Fresno. Then he started out and got as far as this little town of Crampton, which is about thirty or forty miles from Fresno, and there he became ill. I guess actually he became ill before he got there, but when he got to Crampton he didn't have the strength to go on."

"What sort of an illness?" Mason asked.

"Now there, of course, you can't tell for sure. I'm coming to that in a minute. He was a heavy drinker. He had high blood pressure and he had no business drinking, but he'd evidently been drinking and he'd eaten something that disagreed with him. Anyway he became terribly ill. He stopped at this motel at Crampton and asked if there was a doctor in town. The landlady told him there were three and gave him the names. He telephoned one of them, a Dr. Renault. Dr. Renault came out right away and decided that Ed was seriously ill. That was between eight and nine o'clock in the morning.

"Now I have an idea that Ed had stayed in Fresno the night before and had been on something of a bat, probably with some woman. Personally I wouldn't doubt but what she'd slipped him some knockout drops. In any event, he'd been rolled."

"How do you know that?" Mason asked.

"I'm coming to that," she said, "but first I want to tell you about what happened. After Dr. Renault got there Ed had quite a sinking spell. Dr. Renault called and told us we'd better get up there at once, that Ed was very seriously ill. He was so ill that the doctor didn't even want to try moving him to a hospital. The nearest one was at Fresno. He said he was trying to get a nurse, but there was a shortage of nurses and he thought it would be a good plan for Myrna to come up at once and she could help with the nursing."

"Go on," Mason said.

"After seeing you, we took a plane to Fresno, then rented a Drive-Ur-Self car and went down to the motel at Crampton.

"Ed was seriously ill all right. I gathered he'd been vomiting and was in pretty much a state of collapse. The doctor talked with us and left word for us to call if there was any change. He said he'd be back within an hour.

"We remained with Ed for a while, then he dropped off to sleep. He seemed to be resting easier, but he was a pretty sick man all right.

"While he was sleeping, I went to my cabin. Myrna stayed with Ed. Then after I'd cleaned up I went back and took over.

"Almost at once Ed had some sort of a spell. He started to choke and gag and gasped for air.

"I ran out and phoned for the doctor and he came almost at once. He said it was serious and sent me to phone to a drugstore for some medicine.

"Myrna was in the shower, but she said she'd throw on a robe and rush over. By the time she got there it was too late. Ed had passed away.

"Then the doctor showed that Ed must have told him something that aroused his suspicions. He glowered at us, locked up the cabin where Ed's body was and told us that we'd have to wait for the sheriff, the coroner and the district attorney. He said that there were circumstances connected with what had happened so that he couldn't sign a death certificate and that an autopsy would have to be performed. He even intimated that he thought Ed had been murdered."

"So what did you do?"

"Well," she said, "I didn't pay very much attention to all that. As soon as I could decently get away I went across the street to a telephone booth at a service station and called you. Then I came back and tried to comfort Myrna. She wasn't overcome by grief. They were headed for a divorce—had been, that is. Ed had ceased to mean anything to her emotionally. But the whole thing was something of a jolt and I wanted to comfort her. It had been a shocking experience for the poor girl."

"Go on," Mason said.

"Well, the doctor locked up the cabin. He said he was 'sealing up the place' and took us to our cabin and questioned us and then he went to call the coroner.

"I guess it was over an hour when finally the coroner came, accompanied by the deputy district attorney and a representative of the sheriff's office. They made quite a thing out of questioning the doctor and asking questions about knockout drops. The doctor gave them the key to the cabin. The deputy sheriff opened the door, went in there and found that Ed must have regained consciousness, climbed out of the window and driven away."

Mason gave a low whistle.

"That's right," she said, "and the officials certainly were angry about it. It seems they'd had some trouble with this Dr. Renault before. This time they were really burned up."

"What did Dr. Renault say?"

"Dr. Renault stuck by his guns. He said that Ed had been dead, that he knew he was dead. He even intimated that we must have disposed of the body in some way so that an autopsy couldn't be performed. He let it be pretty plain that he thought we were afraid to have an autopsy."

"Go on," Mason said as she stopped. "Tell me the rest of it."

"Well, of course, Dr. Renault kept insisting that the body had been moved, but finally the deputy sheriff, talking around with some of the people in the other cabins, found someone who had seen Ed climb out of the window, get into a car and drive away."

"The deuce!" Mason exclaimed.

"That's right. He must have got quite a bit better. The man said Ed was wearing pajamas, that he slid out of the back window. Some car was parked right behind the cabin. Ed stepped on the starter and drove away. Whatever car it was Ed must have stolen it because his car was still there."

"He was in his pajamas?"

"That's what the man said. He naturally wondered why.

Then he thought perhaps someone was trying to escape a raid or something and—"

"He was close enough to recognize the man he saw," Mason asked, "to identify him from photographs or—?"

"Oh, heavens no. He was a hundred feet away. He just saw the figure of a man, and he's quite certain the figure was wearing pajamas. He said they were dotted with red. And those were Ed's pajamas all right.

"Well, then we tried to get you on the telephone but by that time you had left for Paradise and we didn't know how to reach you. We left word at the San Francisco Airport in case you stopped there but evidently you missed the message. So we waited until we thought you'd be in Paradise and called the number of Ed's phone and you answered."

"Now wait a minute," Mason said, "tell me one other thing. How do you know Ed had been rolled?"

"Oh yes, I was coming to that. The money that was in his clothes was an even forty-five dollars and he had paid for the cabin in the motel with a fifty-dollar bill that had been worn smooth. Ed was a heavy drinker. He knew that he was apt to be rolled and he always carried a fifty-dollar bill under the leather lining in the sole of his right shoe so that if anyone rolled him he'd have get-by money to get home on.

"There wasn't even so much as a nickel in change in his pockets—just that forty-five dollars. That was the change he'd been given after paying five dollars for the cabin."

"But why did he get out of the window?" Mason asked. "And how could he have done that if he was as sick as the doctor claimed?"

"Frankly," she said, "I don't think that doctor is willing to tell what really happened. You know when a man dies a doctor gives a shot of some powerful stimulant directly into the heart. I think Dr. Renault did that with Ed and then didn't wait long enough to see if it took effect. He was too anxious to get out and question us. Something Ed must have said at the last must have convinced the doctor that Ed was blaming his sickness on Myrna in some way.

"Of course the doctor thinks we hid the body and disposed

of it, that it even might have been Myrna who got in through the window, put on pajamas and climbed out again.

"If you ask me I think this doctor saw Ed's heart had stopped and gave him this injection of adrenaline or whatever it is and then went out.

"Ed regained consciousness and that powerful stimulant gave him strength enough to get up and go to the door. When he found it was locked from the outside he got in a panic, crawled out through the window, jumped in the first car he found and drove away.

"It's absurd to think a frail little thing like Myrna could have moved the body. Anyway, why would *we* be afraid of an autopsy? He'd been taken sick long before we got there."

"Where are his things?" Mason asked. "His clothes, his baggage."

"The sheriff's office took charge of everything. The deputy sheriff was still making an official investigation when we left. He had the key to the place and the place was locked up. We drove to Fresno and called you from there. You told us to get to San Francisco, which we did. We'd previously told the deputy sheriff where he could send Ed's belongings when they got done with them."

"Where do you suppose Ed Davenport is?"

She shrugged her shoulders.

"He certainly can't be driving around in his pajamas, with no money, no driving license—"

"They'll do funny things when they've been drinking," she said. "Myrna tells me she's seen Ed just go as crazy as anything when he's coming out of one of those drinking spells."

"He'll be picked up somewhere," Mason insisted.

"Of course he will. The sheriff's office put out an alarm to the State Highway Patrol. They're alerted to be looking for a man in pajamas driving a car. He isn't safe to be on the road."

"Does the doctor think he'll collapse or—?"

"The doctor," Mrs. Ansel said firmly, "thinks he's dead."

43

"And Ed Davenport made some statement to the doctor that caused him to become suspicious about Myrna?"

"Evidently he did. The doctor asked Myrna about the candy."

"What candy?"

"Well, Myrna tells me Ed had these drinking fits. Ordinarily he doesn't care for candy, but he found out that when the craving for alcohol comes on him, if he'll eat a lot of candy sometimes he can get over the awful craving for liquor.

"Now, as nearly as I can figure things out, before he got to Fresno he felt this craving for liquor coming on and he started eating candy. He carried his candy in his bag just in case of having that craving overtake him."

"What sort of candy?" Mason asked.

"Chocolates—the kind that have liquid in the centers—liquid and cherries. Myrna says he'd eat a few of those, and then sometimes the craving for liquor would leave him. But after he once started drinking he'd drink until his system got saturated with alcohol."

Mason said, "All right, I'm going to make a suggestion. There are some seats up in the front of the plane. Miss Street and I are going up there. When we get to Los Angeles I want you and Mrs. Davenport to get off the plane before we do. I want you to take a taxicab out to your home."

"Why? Why not go in the limousine and then take a taxi?"

Mason shook his head. "I don't want you to follow the same route that is taken by the limousine. I want you to take a taxicab."

"Why?"

"Because," Mason told her, "I want to see if you're being followed."

"But why should *we* be followed?"

"Because you may have been traced to San Francisco, and because the sheriff's office at Fresno may have decided to keep an eye on you."

"But why should they? What business is it of theirs? Why, that's absurd! After all, if Ed Davenport went on a binge and some cutie slipped him knockout drops they can't hold Myrna responsible."

"There may be some other angles," Mason said. "From what you tell me the man is in very poor health. From what Dr. Renault says he must have been in a state of shock, a state of shock which caused the doctor to believe the man was dead. Now then, let's suppose Ed Davenport started driving around in his pajamas. He was very apt to collapse and die, or he might have become involved in an accident. If he gets injured, with his resistance down to such a low ebb, the injuries may prove fatal."

"Well, I still don't see how they expect to hold us responsible for his climbing out of that window. That was the doctor's fault. Ed was in this state of shock or exhaustion or whatever it was, and that fool doctor shot that adrenaline or something right into his heart. That's dynamite. They only do that to dead people when there's no hope. It's a last desperate gamble. You'd think the fool would have had sense enough to be *sure* before he left the room."

Mason nodded thoughtfully.

"Of course," she went on, "it made a pretty kettle of fish. And you up there in Paradise thinking Ed was dead. Just think what would have happened if he'd headed back to Paradise and found you going through his things. Crazy as he was he might have done anything! We were terribly afraid you might get into trouble up there."

"I did," Mason said.

"What was it?"

"Nothing particularly serious," Mason said. "I'll tell you both about it when I see what happens after we get to the airport at Los Angeles. In the meantime quit worrying and try and comfort Mrs. Davenport."

"Oh, she's all right now. But, Mr. Mason, we're going to have to do something for her. I'm completely satisfied that Ed Davenport has been going through her money just as fast as he can. She doesn't care a thing in the world about money just so she can grow flowers, and—"

"How much of Delano's estate has been distributed?" Mason interposed.

"Well, there was a partial distribution and—it amounts to

something over a hundred thousand, I guess, and there's more money coming in all the time. In addition to all that Ed Davenport raised some money on a note that she signed with him. He told her it was just a matter of form, but you can't tell *me* any of that sort of stuff! *I* wasn't born yesterday. I think *I* know something about men!''

''I dare say you do,'' Mason said, ''but in the meantime we'll relax until we get to Los Angeles. Then you get in a taxicab and go home, and, if there's nothing new, be at my office by two-thirty in the afternoon.''

Mason got up, tapped Della on the shoulder and led the way to two vacant seats in the front of the plane.

''Well?'' Della Street asked when Mason had seated her by the window and dropped into position in the seat beside her.

''Did you get the story?'' Mason asked.

''Most of it,'' she said. ''Apparently Ed Davenport was on one of his toots and was rolled. He got sick and passed out. The doctor gave him a shot. Davenport came to and found the door locked, so he thought someone was trying to restrain him. He got out of the window, got in somebody's car and went places.''

''What places?'' Mason asked.

''Probably he started home.''

''Not with all of the Highway Patrol being alerted to look for a man driving a car, clad only in pajamas.''

''Well,'' she said, ''what do *you* think?''

Mason smiled. ''A little bit depends on what Paul Drake has found out about that San Bernardino motel, and a great deal depends on what happens when we get to Los Angeles.''

''You think they were followed to San Francisco?''

Mason nodded.

''You think that man reading the newspaper was interested in them?''

''I think he had cop written all over him,'' Mason said. ''However, we may as well get a few minutes' sleep before we land.''

And with that Mason touched the button which slid the seat back into a reclining position.

"Now," Della Street complained, "you've got *me* wide awake."

"Doing what?"

"Thinking over what's happened."

Mason said sleepily, "Wait an hour and a half and you may have a lot more to think over."

Chapter 5

The plane glided to a landing, then taxied up to the airport.

Mason and Della Street watched Sara Ansel and Myrna Davenport walk through the terminal and enter a taxicab.

The cab swung out into the driveway and then into the traffic.

A businesslike car with a tall aerial in the rear pulled out of a parking position and swung in behind the taxicab.

"Well, that does it," Mason said.

"Police?" Della Street asked.

Mason nodded.

"What are they waiting for, why don't they go ahead and make an arrest?" Della Street asked.

"They're trying to establish a pattern of action."

"So what do we do?"

"We now get two taxicabs."

"Two?"

Mason nodded.

"Wouldn't it be cheaper to take one until we get to town?"

"Exactly," Mason said, "but this way is more confusing."

"Do I try to see if I'm being followed?"

"Definitely not," Mason told her. "You're the soul of innocence. You settle back in the cushions. You've had a long, hard day, and you're going home, take a bath and get a few hours' sleep until you feel like coming to the office, or until I call you."

"And in the meantime what will you be doing?"

Mason said, "I'll bathe, shave, change clothes and see what happens."

"You think something is going to happen?"

"I wouldn't be too surprised."

48

"What?"

Mason said, "Well, I might—just might—run out to the Pacific Palisades Motor Court at San Bernardino."

"Why?"

Mason said, "The man in unit thirteen might turn out to know something about Ed Davenport."

"Oh-oh!" she said, and then, after a moment, "Suppose he does. Then what?"

Mason said, "I might talk with him. I'd like to establish a pattern of action myself."

"Won't you be able to get any sleep?"

"I won't if I go out there, but I won't go out there unless Paul Drake reports the cabin is occupied."

"Why not take me with you?"

Mason shook his head firmly. "You, young lady, are going to get a little shut-eye. The party may get rough from now on."

"You don't think there's a simple explanation for this, that Ed Davenport went on a bust and—?"

"There may be a simple explanation," Mason said, "but there are complicating factors. Here's a taxicab, Della. In you go. You have enough money for expenses?"

"Plenty."

"Okay. See you later."

Mason waved good-by to her and stood stretching and yawning, looking at the glow of light above the city.

Another businesslike car with an aerial in the rear slid out from the parking place and followed Della Street's taxicab.

Mason took another cab and, fighting back in almost irresistible impulse, determinedly kept his eyes to the front and never once looked back to see whether or not a police car was following.

Mason paid off the taxi driver in front of his apartment house, went in and took a shower. Then, wrapped in his bathrobe, called the Drake Detective Agency.

The night operator answered the phone.

"This is Perry Mason," he said. "I suppose Paul Drake is wrapped in the arms of Morpheus."

"He was up here until well after midnight," the operator

said. "He said that if you called we were to relay reports that have come in on that San Bernardino job."

"Let's have them," Mason said.

"Unit thirteen," the operator said, "according to the data made available by our operatives in a telephone report, was rented over the telephone from Fresno Sunday night by a man who identified himself as Frank L. Stanton. He said that he was going to be in late Monday, that he wanted a unit and specifically instructed that the unit be left unlocked so he wouldn't have to bother waking the manager and getting a key. He said he might not get in until between two and three o'clock Tuesday morning, that he would want the unit for two consecutive days. He asked how much the price was, was informed that it was six dollars per day, and said that he would go to the telegraph office and wire twelve dollars for two days."

"That was done?" Mason asked.

"That was done."

"And what about Stanton?"

"Up until thirty minutes ago, when the operative telephoned in a report, Stanton hadn't shown up, but here's a development that you'll probably be interested in."

"What is it?"

"Another detective agency is on the job."

"Watching for Stanton?"

"Apparently."

"Who is it?"

"We're not certain yet but we think it's Jason L. Beckemeyer, a private detective from Bakersfield."

"How are you making your identification?" Mason asked.

"By the license number of the automobile. That gave our men the first lead. Then I telephoned in for a description of Beckemeyer and he answers the description of the driver. Fifty-two, five feet seven, weight a hundred and eighty pounds. A short, chunky, barrel-chested individual."

"Any idea what he's after?"

"Apparently just trying to get a line on who comes to unit thirteen."

"They think that's the one he's watching?"

"They can't be certain but they think so. The other units are all occupied."

"Have the men keep on the job," Mason said. "Also send out another operative to tail Beckemeyer. When he quits he'll probably go to a telephone to report. I'd like very much to find out what number he calls. It'll be from a pay station and your man may be able to do something."

"It's pretty difficult to get those telephone numbers, but we'll try."

"Give it a try," Mason said. "Now here's something else. I'm working on a case involving a man by the name of Ed Davenport. He was supposed to have died in Crampton yesterday. The only trouble with that theory is that the corpse climbed out of a window and drove away.

"It becomes important to know where he was and what he did the night before his 'death.' Probably he was in Fresno. The police will be nosing around in a halfhearted sort of way. They'll be looking for a registration of Edward Davenport. In all probability they won't find a thing because he would have been using an assumed name.

"That motel at San Bernardino gives us a clue to his assumed name. It was probably Frank L. Stanton.

"That may give us a head start on the police. Have your correspondent in Fresno start tracing Frank L. Stanton. Put a dozen men on it if you have to. I want results and I want the thing kept completely confidential. Can do?"

"Can do," she said. "We work with a good outfit at Fresno."

"Okay," Mason told her. "I'll be in my office sometime around ten o'clock, but call me at my apartment if anything important develops."

Mason shaved, had a drink of warm milk, stretched out on a davenport with the morning paper, covered himself with a blanket, read for ten or fifteen minutes, then dozed off into slumber, from which he was awakened by the sharp, insistent ringing of the telephone bell.

Since only Paul Drake and Della Street had the number of his unlisted private phone in the apartment, Mason grabbed for the receiver, said, "Hello."

51

Paul Drake's voice was sharply incisive.

"You're usually waking me up out of a sound sleep, Perry. Now it's your turn."

"Shoot," Mason said, "but I hope it's important."

"It is if you're representing Myrna Davenport. My night operator said you were working on the Ed Davenport case."

"What about it?"

"Myrna Davenport's arrested and is being questioned about a murder."

"Whose murder?"

"Two murders. Ed Davenport, her husband, and Hortense Paxton, her cousin."

"How come?"

"A secret order of exhumation was made day before yesterday. The body of Hortense Paxton was disinterred. She was the niece of William C. Delano. She died a short time before he did, and—"

"Yes, yes," Mason said. "I know all about that. Go on, what about it?"

"They found enough arsenic in the body to kill a horse. There seems to be no question that she died of arsenic poisoning, although a physician signed it out as a natural death."

"And what about Mrs. Davenport?"

"Picked up for questioning on that murder and also on orders from Fresno for the murder of her husband."

"Have they found his body?"

"The husband's?"

"Yes."

"Not yet, but they seem to have uncovered some new evidence up there. At first they thought a doctor had made a mistake. They gave him hell but he stuck by his guns and now he seems to have them pretty well convinced the man was murdered."

"Then the body climbed out through a window and drove away," Mason said. "That's a pretty active corpse if you ask me."

"Well, I don't know all the details. I'm just telling you what I know."

"Where is Mrs. Davenport?"

"Picked up by the local police, but she *may* have been flown to Fresno for questioning there."

"Have you found out anything about Davenport's last night in Fresno, where he stayed—probably under the name of Stanton?"

"Not yet, Perry, but we're working on it. Now here's the problem, Perry. Here's where all this begins to get pretty close to you. You may lose a little hide over this one."

"Shoot," Mason said.

"Davenport, you know, had the business office of his mining company up in Paradise. So the police telephoned the sheriff of Butte County at Oroville and the sheriff went up to Paradise to make an investigation.

"Then he found out that you had been up there last night, that you'd been in the place, apparently taking charge of things for the widow. There was an envelope that Davenport had left to be opened in the event of his death.

"The sheriff's office opened the envelope. In it they found six sheets of blank paper. They submitted the envelope to an expert who states that the envelope had been steamed open within the last twenty-four hours and resealed with mucilage.

"You can figure out where that leaves you. I thought I'd wake you up and let you know because you may be in a position where you have to answer some embarrassing questions."

"When?"

"As soon as they can locate you. This angle is hot as a stove lid. They think you found accusations that named your client as a poisoner and destroyed the original letter, substituting those blank sheets of paper."

"Mrs. Davenport has been formally arrested?" Mason asked.

"That's right."

"What about Sara Ansel?"

"No charge against her. Della Street wanted me to tell you that she's been haunting the office but Della has been holding her off—"

"Della?" Mason said. "Is she at the office?"

"Bright and early," Drake said. "She opened up at nine o'clock."

"The devil!" Mason exclaimed. "I told her to get some sleep. What time is it now?"

"Ten o'clock. Della thought you'd be wanting to sleep so she went up to open the office and filter things through so that you wouldn't be disturbed except on a matter of urgency."

"Does she know about this?"

"Not all of it," Drake said. "I called you first. I'm going down the hall and tell her about it as soon as I hang up."

Mason said, "Tell her I'll be at the office within twenty or twenty-five minutes."

"Provided the authorities don't pick you up for questioning," Drake reminded him.

"Tell her I'll be up within twenty or twenty-five minutes," Mason repeated and hung up.

Mason hurriedly dressed, left his apartment house by a back exit, and hurried to his office. He hesitated for a moment at the door of the Drake Detective Agency, then decided to see Della Street first and walked rapidly down the corridor. He fitted his latchkey to the door of his private office and went in.

Della Street saw him and placed a warning finger on her lips. She hurriedly closed the doors to the law library and the connecting office, then lowered her voice and said, "Chief, we have a bear by the tail."

"How come?"

"Wait until you hear Sara Ansel's story."

"What about her?"

"She's fit to be tied."

"Why?"

"She's suddenly found out that Myrna Davenport wasn't the sweet, passive little thing she thought."

"*How* did she find out?"

"She wants to tell you. Chief, you aren't really obligated to represent Mrs. Davenport in this case. This is a murder case. Your agreement with her was to represent her in the estate matter and—"

54

Mason interrupted with a shake of his head.

"No?" Della asked.

"No," Mason said. "When I take a client I stay with that client."

"I know," she said, "but—well, wait until you talk with Sara Ansel."

"You've talked with her?"

"Generally."

"How does it look?"

"Bad."

"All right," Mason said, "suppose Myrna's guilty. She's at least entitled to a fair representation. She's entitled to her day in court. She's entitled to her constitutional rights. She's entitled to be confronted with the witnesses against her and to have them cross-examined. But somehow I can't feel this case is as black as it seems."

"It couldn't be," Della Street said. "Do you want to talk with Mrs. Ansel now?"

"Bring her in," Mason said. "Why didn't you get some sleep, Della?"

"Because I wanted to be on the job so *you* could get some rest. I can catch forty winks after lunch. If you get mixed up in this thing you're *really* going to be busy. And there are several long-distance calls. Among them a call from the district attorney of Butte County."

"I wonder what *he* wants," Mason said, and then smiled.

"Yes," Della Street remarked demurely, "I wonder."

"Well, let's take things one at a time," Mason said. "I'm in conference at the moment. I can't be disturbed by any calls. I'll be available in thirty minutes. Now let's see what Mrs. Ansel has to say."

Della Street nodded, picked up the phone and said to Gertie at the switchboard, "Mr. Mason is in now, Gertie. Tell Mrs. Ansel he'll see her at once. I'm coming out to escort her in."

Della Street left the office and returned with Sara Ansel, who had ceased all pretext of keeping herself well groomed. Her face was haggard and tired. There were swollen pouches under her eyes. Such make-up as she was wearing had been hastily applied and it was quite apparent she had had no sleep.

"Mr. Mason," she said, crossing the office toward him and literally grabbing his hand, "you *must* do something. We've got to extricate ourselves from this thing. It's terrible."

"Sit down," Mason said. "Calm yourself. Tell me just what happened."

"Everything's happened."

"Well," Mason said, "tell me about it."

"I can never forgive myself. I can never forgive myself for being such a fool. I let that little minx pull the wool right over my eyes and . . . and then I got you into it. I thought I knew something about human nature, and in the relatively short time I had known her that woman became almost like a daughter to me. She seemed so helpless, so imposed upon, so frightfully inadequate to cope with the situation. And now to think of what has happened."

"Go on," Mason said. "Tell me about it. You may not have too much time, you know."

"Why that woman is a regular Lucrezia Borgia. She's a minx, a poisoner, a murderess."

"*Please* give me the facts," Mason said, seating himself and studying Sara Ansel.

"Well," she said, "to begin with the coroner exhumed the body of Hortense Paxton. He found she'd been poisoned. Myrna Davenport did it."

"When did you learn all this?"

"Well, it all started when we got home. There was a notice of a telegram under the door. Myrna called the telegraph office and it seems some friend of hers had sent a telegram that said to call immediately, no matter what hour of the day or night."

"Go on," Mason said.

"So Myrna called and this friend told her that the coroner had exhumed the body and was taking the stomach and organs for an analysis."

"And then what?"

She said, "Believe me, Mr. Mason, I have never been so

completely shocked in my life. Myrna stood there just as demure and quiet as anything, and then said, 'Aunt Sara, before I sleep I want to do a little work in the garden.' "

Mason raised his eyebrows.

"She's a great little gardener," Sara Ansel explained. "That was her only recreation. But—well, wait until you hear *what* that woman was doing."

"I'm waiting," Mason reminded her.

"I was just completely all in," Mrs. Ansel went on. "I'm not young enough and resilient enough to go tearing around on these trips, taking all this excitement and experiencing all of these night plane rides. I was about ready to fall on my face, but I decided to take a hot shower and then get into bed. I went up to my room, showered, and—well, I'd better explain that that room is on the second story and it looks down on the yard in back of the patio, and *what* do you think I saw Myrna Davenport doing?"

"What was she doing?" Mason asked impatiently.

"Calmly proceeding to dig a hole, a very deep hole. She wasn't gardening at all. She had a spade and she was digging a hole."

"Go on," Mason said.

"And right while I was watching her she took some packages, little paper packages, and dumped them in the hole and then proceeded to cover the packages with dirt. After she'd filled the hole with dirt she took sod that she had cut out and carefully patted the sod back into place, making a good smooth job of it."

"And then?" Mason asked.

"Well, all that time I was standing at the window watching her. I'm not nosy, Mr. Mason, but I *do* have a normal, healthy, human curiosity."

"So what did you do?"

"So I marched right downstairs and caught that demure little hypocrite before she'd had a chance to get rid of the spade."

"What happened?"

"I asked her what she'd been doing and she said that when she got nervous she always liked to be out with her flowers, that she'd been spading up around some of the plants, loosening the soil and getting them so they could enjoy a new day, and now she was thoroughly relaxed and she could go in, go to sleep and sleep for twelve hours."

"And what did you say?"

"I asked her to show me where she'd been spading, and she said that that wasn't important and besides I should get in the house and get some sleep."

"And then what?"

"I insisted that I wanted to see where she'd been spading. I told her that I wanted to see how she did it."

"Well?" Mason asked.

"She'd given me the impression, Mr. Mason, of being a demure little thing, a meek little woman who could be pushed around, but you should have seen her then. She was just as obstinate as a brick wall. She wouldn't look at me, but she didn't budge an inch. She said in that low voice of hers that it really wasn't important and that I was upset and nervous because of my night's trip and that I should go back into the house."

"And then what?"

"So then I came right out and asked her why she lied to me. I asked her why she had dug that hole, and she told me she hadn't dug a hole."

"What did you do?"

"So with that I snatched the shovel out of her hands and marched out across the patio to the lawn and over to the exact place where she'd been digging."

"And then?" Mason asked.

"Then for the first time she was willing to admit what she had been doing, but there was no shame about her and she didn't even raise her voice. She said, 'Aunt Sara, don't do that,' and I asked her why not and she said, 'Because I've been very careful to replace the sod over that hole so that no one will notice it. If you tamper with it, it's going to make it obvious that something has been buried there.' "

"And then?"

"So then I asked her what she'd buried, and what do you think she told me?"

"What?"

"Little packages of arsenic and cyanide of potassium. Now isn't *that* nice?"

"Go on," Mason said.

"Well, the little minx had the audacity to stand there and tell me that she had been experimenting with different types of spray for pests on flowers, that she had some 'active ingredients,' as she called them, that were very poisonous. The arsenic she had purchased. Some of the cyanide of potassium she had got from the laboratory in her husband's mining operations. She'd been experimenting with different types of plant sprays for killing various pests, and now she was afraid her action in collecting those poisons might be subject to question, just in case someone started looking around with the idea of poison in mind. She said under the circumstances she thought she'd better get rid of the stuff."

"So what did you do?" Mason asked.

"I suppose I should have had my head examined. I believed her. She never raised her voice and was so sweet and demure and so completely unexcited that I let her convince me. I even got to feeling sorry for her again. I sympathized with her and told her I couldn't understand how she could go through so much and not be hysterical.

"Well, I put my arm around her and we walked back to the house, and I went upstairs and went to bed, and I was just getting to sleep when there was this pounding on the door and the housekeeper came up to tell us that an officer was there, that he had to see us right away upon a matter of the greatest importance."

"And what was the matter of greatest importance?"

"It seemed that the coroner's chemist had found arsenic in Hortie's body, and the district attorney wanted to question Myrna."

"Then what?"

"So then they took Myrna up to the district attorney's office."

"And you?"

"Nothing was done with me," she said. "They asked me how long I'd been there and I told them. They asked me a few questions and then they took Myrna up to the district attorney's office."

"How did Myrna take it?" Mason asked.

"Just like she takes everything," Sara said. "She was quiet and mouselike. Her voice didn't raise a bit. She said that she'd be glad to go to the district attorney's office but she thought she should have a little sleep, that she'd been up all night on account of her husband's illness."

"And then?" Mason asked.

"That's all I know. They took her away. But I began to start putting two and two together, and then I got to thinking about that candy that Ed Davenport had in his bag. You know, Mr. Mason, she told me that she packs his bag every time he goes away. She said he was helpless—didn't know how to fold his clothes and all of that."

"That's not unusual," Mason said. "Most wives do that for their husbands."

"I know, but that meant she must have packed the candy, so I started looking around after she left. I just started looking things over a little bit and—"

"What were you looking for?" Mason asked.

"Oh, just things that would help."

"You went into her room?"

"Well, yes."

"And what did you find?"

"I found a box of candy in her bureau similar to the kind of candy that Ed Davenport carries with him when he travels—those cherries that are in chocolate with sweet syrup around them. She has a sweet tooth herself. I remember a couple of boxes of that same type of candy had been hanging around the living room, and Myrna had kept asking *me* to help her eat them up. I only had a couple of pieces because I'm watching my figure. However, you can see what it means—the significance of it all.

"Good heavens, suppose she'd been trying to poison me! Suppose one of the pieces of candy she offered me had been poisoned! It must have been fate that guided my hand to the right pieces.

"And then she kept insisting I have more. I didn't take

any on account of my figure, but you can see what she must have had in mind. I thought at the time she was unduly insistent.

"Looking back at it now, I can see that the little minx must have been pulling the wool over my eyes all along.

"I can think of a lot of little things now that had seemed trivial at the time, but now they all begin to fit into a pattern. She's a murderess, a poisoner, a regular Lucrezia Borgia."

Mason thought things over for a few seconds, then said, "Let me ask you a few questions. As I understand it, you two women were together *all* of the time you were there in Crampton. You—"

"Oh no, that's not true. She was alone with Ed while I was taking a shower. Then, shortly after the doctor reported that Ed had passed away and locked up the place, I went to telephone you. Now I remember seeing her talking with some man as I started back toward the cabin. Then she and the man separated. I didn't think much of it at the time because I thought perhaps it was just one of the other tenants who was expressing his sympathy, but now I know it could have been a male accomplice. He probably entered the cabin through the window. After he got in there he was smart enough to put on a pair of pajamas. He must have slipped Ed's body out through the window and into his own automobile. Then he waited until he was certain someone was looking, climbed back out of the window again, got in his automobile and drove away."

"Your feelings seem to have changed all of a sudden," Mason said.

"Well, I'll certainly say they have. Why wouldn't they? The scales have dropped from my eyes, Mr. Mason."

"Thank you very much for telling me."

"What are you going to do?" Sara Ansel asked.

"I don't know yet."

"Well, I know what *I'm* going to do. *I'm* going to clear my skirts. I'm going to maintain my good name and my reputation."

"I see," Mason said. "I suppose that will include going to the police?"

"I'm not going to the police but I'm certainly not going to avoid them when they come to me."

"And what are you going to tell them about me?" Mason asked.

"You mean about going up to Paradise to get that letter?" Mason nodded.

She met his eyes grimly and uncompromisingly. "I'm going to tell them the truth."

"I thought perhaps you would," Mason announced dryly.

"I don't think your attitude is being co-operative, Mr. Mason."

"I'm an attorney and I only co-operate with my clients."

"Your clients! You mean you're still going to represent that woman after what she did to you, after the position in which she put you, after the lies she told you, after the—?"

"I'm going to represent her," Mason said. "At least I'm going to see that she has her day in court and isn't convicted of anything except by due process of law."

"Well, of all the fools!" Sara Ansel snapped. She got up out of the chair, stood glowering at Mason for a moment, then said, "I might have known I was wasting my time."

With that she turned and strode toward the exit door. She jerked it open, looked back over her shoulder and said, "And I was trying to help you!"

She walked out into the corridor.

Mason watched the closing door. "That," he said to Della Street, "is what comes when an attorney accepts the obvious."

"What do you mean?"

"A client's statement to an attorney is a confidential communication," Mason explained. "An attorney's clerk or secretary can be present at the conversation and it's still confidential. The law gives that protection. But when a third person is present the communication ceases to be confidential."

"But, good Lord, Chief, this was a woman who came with her, a woman whom she brought along and—"

"I know," Mason said. "At the time Mrs. Davenport thought it was to her best interest to have Sara Ansel with her. I was the attorney. I should have insisted that the conversation about that letter take place in private."

"And since it didn't? Then what?"

"Since it didn't," Mason said, "it isn't a privileged communication."

"And you mean you can't avoid answering questions about it?"

"Not when those questions are asked by the proper persons in the proper forum under proper authorization," Mason said.

"And until then?"

"Until then," Mason told her, "I don't have to answer a damn thing."

"So what do we do about the district attorney of Butte County?" Della Street asked.

"Oh, we talk with him by all means. Tell the operator that I'm ready to take his call now."

Della Street busied herself on the telephone and a moment later nodded to Perry Mason, who picked up the phone, said in his most formal voice, "Perry Mason speaking."

The voice that came over the wire sounded slightly forced, as though a man might be trying to mask a certain amount of diffidence by excessive vigor. "I am Jonathan Halder, Mr. Mason. I'm the district attorney of Butte County and I want to question you, and your secretary, about a visit you made up here to Paradise."

"Indeed," Mason said cordially. "I'm mighty glad to meet you, Mr. Halder, even over the telephone, but I don't know why you would want to question us on what I consider a very routine matter of business."

"Well, it may not be so routine," Halder said. "Now we can get at it the easy way or we can get at it the hard way."

"The hard way?" Mason asked.

Halder kept the forced vigor in his voice. "I have the right of course to take the entire matter before the grand jury and—"

"What matter?" Mason asked.

"The matter that brought you up here and what you did."

"Good Lord, man," Mason interrupted with all the geniality of one talking to an old friend, "if, for any reason, you have any official interest in anything that Miss Street and I did in your county we'll be only too glad to answer questions. You won't have to bother with a grand jury or a subpoena or trying to resort to any legal formalities—"

"Well, I'm mighty glad to hear you say that!" Halder interrupted, his voice relaxing into a more normal tone. "I guess perhaps I've misjudged you. People up here told me you were pretty resourceful and pretty ingenious, that if you didn't want to be interrogated I might have to go the limit, even to the extent of getting out a warrant."

Mason threw back his head and laughed. "Well, well, well," he said. "One's reputation certainly can get distorted with distance, like a mirage. How important is all this, Mr. Halder? When do you want to see me?"

"I'm afraid it's *very* important, and I want to see you as soon as possible."

"I'm rather busy at the moment," Mason said.

Once more a strained note crept into Halder's voice. "It is *very* important, Mr. Mason, not only on account of the situation here but because I am co-operating with other law enforcement officers and it's pretty generally agreed that we want—"

"Certainly, certainly. I understand," Mason said, laughing again. "You get in a political office and they start putting the pressure on you and then I suppose someone blabs to the newspapers and the first thing you know you're on a spot. It's either up to you to get me there for questioning or be subject to a lot of criticism."

Halder, his voice easy and informal once more, said, "You must be psychic, Mr. Mason, or else you've been a district attorney in a relatively small community."

"Well," Mason said, "I'm pretty busy, but Miss Street and I can get up there all right. Now, let's see. I'll catch a plane to San Francisco and then—"

"Our plane service leaves something to be desired," Halder said.

"That's all right," Mason told him. "I'm too busy to bother with waiting for scheduled planes. Tell you what I'll do, Halder. I'll get up to San Francisco or perhaps to Sacramento, then I'll charter a plane. You have a landing field at Oroville?''

"Oh yes.''

"All right,'' Mason said. "I'll be on that landing field at five-thirty right on the dot.''

"Oh, you don't need to break your neck trying to get here at a certain specified time,'' Halder said. "I want to talk with you, and of course I'd like to talk with you as soon as possible, but—''

"That's all right,'' Mason said. "You're a busy man. You have things to do. I'm a busy man. I have things to do. We may just as well make a definite appointment so that you'll know when to expect me and I'll know that when I arrive there won't be any time lost in getting together. Will five-thirty be all right?''

"That will be fine,'' Halder said, and then added apologetically, "I dislike very much to bother a man who is as busy as you are and whose time is as valuable. After all, it's probably only relatively a minor matter—that is, I mean you certainly have an explanation, but—well, I've been under considerable pressure and—''

"I understand,'' Mason said cordially. "Think nothing of it, Halder. I'm glad to do it. Miss Street and I will be there at five-thirty.''

Mason hung up the telephone and grinned at Della Street.

"Chief,'' she said, "you certainly gave up without a struggle on that one.''

Mason said, "Let's be practical, Della.''

"Is that being practical?''

He nodded.

"I don't get it.''

Mason said, "Things are pretty hot for us at the moment. I'd like to avoid being questioned as long as possible.''

"Well,'' she said.

"And,'' Mason told her, "that means I don't want to be available for the local press, the local police or the local district attorney. I want a little time to correlate my thoughts and, above all, I want a little time for some of the seed we have planted to start sprouting. I want to find out what Paul Drake can uncover.''

"And so,'' she said, ''you walk right into the arms of the district attorney up at Butte County where you certainly don't dare to answer certain questions without putting your neck in a noose.''

"The more questions I answer right now the more I'm apt to get my neck in a noose,'' Mason said. ''But just stop to think of the practical realities, and the beauty of this situation will occur to you, Della.

"In the first place we can leave immediately and in a rush. We don't have time to answer questions asked by anybody. We're hurrying to catch a plane in order to keep an appointment with the district attorney of Butte County. We get a lot of publicity which is bound to be favorable because it means that as soon as we learned the district attorney wanted to question us we dropped everything and dashed up to his county without forcing him to resort to any last desperate measures.

"We fix a definite time of arrival which is such that we can be comfortably hurried. We're away from the office. We don't need to let anyone know where we are. They can't call it flight because we're on our way to confer with the authorities in Butte County at their request.

"Moreover, Della, because we have a definite time of arrival, and because the Butte County papers are hungry for news, we go up and make news. Since we have fixed a definite time of arrival, the press can be there with photographers.''

"I can see the beauty of all that,'' Della Street said. ''It's a wonderful respite for five or six hours. But what happens when we arrive in Butte County?''

"That,'' Mason said, ''is a question I wish I could answer.''

"Are you going to answer questions as to just what we did in that house in Paradise?''

"Heaven forbid.''

"How are you going to avoid answering them?''

"I wish I knew,'' Mason told her. ''Come on, Della, get

started. I have to take a few minutes to look up some law, and then we'll be on our way. Get us plane reservations while I do some quick research.''

Chapter 6

The plane they had chartered at Sacramento passed the Marysville buttes on the left and the peculiar, distinctive mountain formation back of Oroville began to show plainly. Table mountains rose nearly a thousand feet above the surrounding country, level as a floor on top. There some huge prehistoric lava flow had covered the whole country, then gradually, as small crevices had offered drainage, the process of interminable erosion had chiseled small cracks into valleys. Now the level of the whole surrounding country had been eroded hundreds of feet, leaving those places where the lava cap had protected the undersoil as veritable table mountains.

Della Street looked at her wrist watch. "We'll make it right on the nose," she said.

Mason nodded.

"And we haven't been very badly hurried at that."

"And," Mason pointed out, "we haven't been interrogated. So far no one has found out just where we are."

"Will the Los Angeles press intimate that you have run away to avoid questioning?" she asked.

"No. They'll find out we're headed for Oroville. They'll ask the local reporters to cover the story and give it to the wire services. They'll state that we are presently unavailable but be forced to explain we are co-operating with the officials up north."

The plane dipped forward and started losing altitude.

"Pretty quick," Della said, "*you're* going to have to devise a way of avoiding answers."

Mason nodded.

"How are you going to do it?"

"I can't tell until I hear the questions."

"Well," she said, "you got a little sleep on the plane anyway."

"How did you do, Della?"

"Pretty fair, but I'm too worried to sleep much."

Mason said, "Let them interrogate me first. If they should try to interrogate you separately, tell them that because you're my secretary you feel that all questions should first be answered by me, that you will answer questions covering subjects on which I have answered questions, but that you don't want to be placed in the position of answering questions on subjects that I may have chosen to consider as privileged. And inasmuch as you're not an attorney and therefore don't understand the legal distinctions you prefer to have me make the decisions."

"How much of what we did, how much of what we know, what we said and what was told us is privileged?" she asked.

Mason made a little gesture with his shoulders, took a notebook from his pocket. "That, of course, is a question.

"The authorities aren't uniform on the subject. In the case of Gallagher versus Williamson, 23 Cal. 331, it was held generally that statements made by a client in the presence of other persons are not privileged and the attorney is bound to disclose them. Later on, in the case of People versus Rittenhouse, 56 C.A. 541, it was held that a third person who was not within the classification of a confidential relation and who overheard communications between an attorney and a client could disclose what he had heard. Then again, in People versus White, 102 C.A. 647, it was held that communications between an attorney and his clients in the presence of third persons were not privileged communications. However, there was a question in that case as to whether the communications were intended to be of a confidential nature. The court held generally that an attorney could be made to testify as to conversations which he had with the defendants in the presence of third persons.

"A much later case was that of People versus Hall 55 C.A. 2d, 343, wherein it was held that communications between an attorney and client in the presence of a third person were not privileged. I've been kicking myself for letting Sara Ansel sit in on that conversation."

"But, Chief, you couldn't have been expected to anticipate any development such as this."

"Why not?" Mason asked. "An attorney is supposed to anticipate not only the things that may happen but the things that can happen. It's not at all unreasonable that two women are going to have a falling-out, and when there's no real reason for a third person to be present an attorney shouldn't—"

"But, good Lord, Chief, *she* had to do all the talking. Myrna Davenport never would have told you the story."

Mason said, "She could speak English. She didn't need an interpreter. Of course, Sara Ansel stepped into the dominant role."

The plane skimmed over the city of Oroville, flying low so that it was possible to see the big, roomy houses occupying strategic positions under towering shade trees.

"What beautiful trees," Della Street said. "You can see how large they are, flying over them like this."

"It gets hot here in the summer," Mason said. "Nature compensates for it by making it a paradise for shade trees. Fig trees grow to enormous heights and give dense shade. Well, here we are, Della. Brace yourself for a barrage."

The plane banked sharply, circled into a landing, and taxied up to the airport.

A group of men came hurrying toward the plane. In the vanguard were newspaper photographers with cameras and flashlights held in readiness. Behind them, moving at a more dignified pace but nevertheless hurrying, was a group of purposeful men.

Alighting from the plane, Mason and Della Street were most considerate in their posing so as to give the photographers plenty of coverage.

Newspaper reporters produced folded newsprint and pencils, ready to report the interview.

One of the reporters bustled forward. "May I have your name please?" he asked.

"Perry Mason," Mason said, smiling.

"Your full name?"

"Perry Mason."

"And you?" he asked, turning to Della Street.

"Miss Della Street."

"You're Mr. Mason's confidential secretary?"

"Yes."

"Thank you," the reporter said, and shook hands with Mason.

"Quite all right," Mason said, and then suddenly the smile froze momentarily on his face as he realized that the reporter had slipped a piece of folded paper into his hand.

Mason hastily shoved his right hand into his coat pocket and smiled at the youngish, rather fleshy individual who pushed his way forward.

"Mr. Halder?" Mason asked.

"That's right. I'm the district attorney, and this is the sheriff of the county. I also have one of my deputies present. I'd like to drive at once to my office if you don't mind, Mr. Mason."

"I'm glad to do anything I can to accommodate," Mason said.

"We have a county car here and we'll get you to the office and terminate the interview just as rapidly as possible."

Mason said, "It's all right. My pilot is authorized to do instrument flying so he tells me we can go back any time tonight."

"I'm sorry that it was necessary for you to go to the expense of chartering a plane, Mr. Mason, but—well, there wasn't much *I* could do about it. We try to keep the expenses of administering the office down to a minimum."

"I can readily understand," Mason said breezily. "Think nothing of it."

Halder turned to the newspaper reporters. "Now I'm sorry to disappoint you boys, but I don't want you to stand here and throw questions at Mr. Mason. I'd like to conduct the inquiry in my own way. After that I'll issue a statement to the press, or the reporters can be called in—unless Mr. Mason has some objection."

"I never have any objection to the press," Mason said,

smiling genially. "I share all of my information with them—except, of course, that which is confidential or which for strategic reasons I feel cannot be divulged."

"Well, that's fine," Halder said, "and we certainly appreciate your co-operation, Mr. Mason. I can't begin to tell you how *much* we appreciate it. Now if you and Miss Street will just get right in the car. And please, boys, no questions until after the interview at my office."

Mason said, "Just a minute. I may have a wire I want to send."

He pulled a billfold from his breast pocket, opened it, studied the interior for a moment, then dropped his right hand to his side pocket, brought out the folded slip of paper the newspaper reporter had placed in his hand, and managed to spread that slip over the interior of the billfold so that he could read the message which had been typed on the paper. It read:

I am Pete Ingram, reporter for *The Oroville Mercury*. Mabel Norge, secretary to Ed Davenport, is missing. I've been unable to find her all day. No one knows where she is. Yesterday afternoon she drew out nearly all the money in Davenport's account in the Paradise bank. Don't ask me how I know because it's a confidential tip. I'm slipping this to you because I'm hoping the information may be of some value to you. You can reciprocate by giving me a break.

Mason folded the billfold, tucking the message inside, put it back in his pocket, and looked over the heads of the little group of men until he encountered the questioning eyes of Pete Ingram.

Mason gave an all but imperceptible nod.

"Well, if you want to send a telegram," Halder said, "we can—"

"Oh, I guess it can wait," Mason told him. "After all, we won't be here very long I take it."

"I hope not," Halder said fervently.

Mason and Della Street entered the automobile. The sheriff sat up front with Halder, who did the driving. The deputy district attorney, whose name was Oscar Glencoe, an older man than Halder, sat quietly, uncommunicative, on the left rear seat. Della Street occupied the center, and Mason sat on the right.

The county car roared into speed and Halder drove directly to the courthouse.

"If you don't mind," he told Mason, "we'll hold the interview in the sheriff's private office."

"Anyplace suits me," Mason said cheerfully.

They disembarked and the sheriff led the way into his private office where chairs had been carefully arranged around the desk. Mason, looking the place over, felt certain that there was a concealed microphone and a tape recorder.

"Well, sit down," the sheriff invited. "Jon, do you want to sit there at the desk and ask the questions?"

"Thank you," Jonathan Halder said and seated himself in the swivel chair at the desk.

The others seated themselves and Halder carefully waited for the last noise of the scraping chairs before asking the first question—further indication that the interview was being recorded.

Halder cleared his throat, took a folded document from his pocket, spread it on the table in front of him, said, "Mr. Mason, you and your secretary, Miss Street, wcrc at Paradise yesterday evening."

"Let's see," Mason said, thinking. "Was it only yesterday? I guess that's right, Counselor. So much has been happening it seems as though it must have been the day before. No, I guess it was yesterday. That was the twelfth—Monday. That's right."

"And you entered the house of Edward Davenport on Crestview Drive?"

"Well, now," Mason said, smiling affably, "I notice you're reading those questions, Mr. Halder. I take it then that this is somewhat in the nature of a formal interrogation."

"Does that make any difference?" Halder asked pleasantly.

"Oh, a lot of difference," Mason said. "If we're just chatting informally that's one thing, but if you're asking formal questions from a list which you have carefully prepared I'll have to be careful in thinking of my answers."

"Why?" Halder asked, instantly suspicious. "Isn't the truth the same in any event?"

"Why certainly," Mason told him, "but take, for instance, this last question of yours. You asked me if I entered the house of Edward Davenport."

"And that, of course, can be answered yes or no," Halder said, his manner watchful.

"No," Mason said. "It's not that easy."

"Why not?"

"Let's put it this way. If this is going to be a formal interview, I'll have to be very careful to make my statements one hundred per cent accurate."

"Well, that's what I want, and I assume that's what you want too."

"Therefore," Mason said, "I would have to state that I entered a house which belonged to *Mrs*. Edward Davenport."

"Now wait a minute," Halder said. "That house was where Ed Davenport was carrying on his business and—"

"That's just the point," Mason interrupted. "That's the point I'm trying to make."

"I don't get you."

"Don't you see? If you were talking informally and asked me if I entered Ed Davenport's place up there why I'd say casually and offhand, 'Sure I did,' but if this is a formal interview and you ask me if I entered the house belonging to Ed Davenport then I have to stop and think. I have a lot of things to take into consideration. I have to say to myself, 'Now I am representing Myrna Davenport, who is the widow of Edward Davenport. If the house was community property she actually gained complete title to it at the moment Ed Davenport died. If the house was separate property but a will left everything to Myrna Davenport then my client acquired title instantly upon Ed Davenport's death, subject only to probate administration. Therefore if I should say in a *formal* interview that I had entered a house belonging to Ed Davenport, it might be considered as an admission I knew about a will but doubted the validity of the will or that I was willing to concede as Mrs. Davenport's attorney that it was not community property. See my point, Counselor?"

Halder seemed perplexed. "I see your point, Mr. Mason, but, good Lord, you're splitting a lot of legal hairs."

"Well, if you're going to draw a hairline distinction with formal questions," Mason said, "I see nothing else for me to do except split the hairs when I think they are divisible."

Mason's smile was completely disarming.

Halder said, "I'd like to have you answer the questions informally, Mr. Mason."

"Well, now," Mason said, "that poses a problem. After all, I'm Mrs. Davenport's attorney. I don't know yet whether there's going to be a criminal action against her. I understand there may be. In that event I'm an attorney representing her in a criminal action. I am also her attorney representing her interest in probating the estate of her husband. Presumably that includes community property and perhaps some separate property. There is the relationship of husband and wife and there may be the relationship under a will. It is quite possible that if you ask me questions from a written list at this time so that your questions can be recalled at any subsequent date and repeated in their exact phraseology, some of my answers might jeopardize the interests of my client. I might, for instance, run up against the question of whether she murdered her husband, Ed Davenport. That, I take it, is conceivable under the circumstances, isn't it, Counselor?"

"I don't know," Halder said shortly. "I refuse to make any predictions as to what action will be taken by the officials in other jurisdictions."

Mason said, "I believe you stated over the telephone that you were being subjected to some pressure."

"That's right."

"Pressure, I take it, from the law enforcement agencies in other counties."

"Yes."

"And quite obviously that pressure was not brought to

bear upon you simply because of the possibility of an unlawful or unauthorized entry on the premises of Edward Davenport in Paradise, California. That pressure was brought to bear on you because someone feels that Ed Davenport is dead and that there is a possibility—mind you, Counselor, I am now talking entirely about the state of mind of the person or persons who brought pressure to bear on you—that there is a possibility Mrs. Davenport had something to do with the death of Edward Davenport. Isn't that right?''

"I'm afraid I shouldn't answer that question frankly, Mr. Mason."

Mason said suavely, ''Now it is my understanding of the law that if a person murders another person, that person cannot inherit any property from the decedent. Isn't that your understanding, Counselor?''

"Exactly."

"So," Mason said, "suppose that you should ask me a question which would involve ownership to certain property—that is, the question of the status of the present title to that property, and suppose further it should be property which Ed Davenport owned in his lifetime, which he left to his wife under the terms of a will which would be perfectly valid on its face and which under ordinary circumstances would have passed title to the property to his widow. Then suppose I should, inadvertently mind you, in my answer indicate that the property did not at the present time belong to Mrs. Davenport, then it is quite possible that someone—not you, of course, Counselor, because I know you are too ethical to take advantage of a mere slip of that sort—but someone who was more technically minded would use that statement as an indication of the fact that I had admitted that Mrs. Davenport was guilty of the murder and therefore couldn't take title and hadn't taken title."

Mason sat back, smiled at the three puzzled interrogators and took a cigarette case from his pocket.

"Anybody care to smoke?" he asked.

There was silence.

Mason extracted a cigarette, tapped it on the side of the

cigarette case, lit up, blew out a cloud of smoke and fairly beamed at the interrogators.

"Well, now wait a minute," Halder said. "I've started to question you and it seems that about all I'm doing is answering questions."

"Of course," Mason said, "I want to have the status of the interview plainly determined. I'm asking you now, Counselor, as one attorney to the other, what do you think? Should I say anything that would intimate in any way that I thought my client was not eligible to succeed to the estate of the dead husband?"

"Certainly not. No one's asking you to."

"Exactly," Mason said. "Therefore when you ask me about a question of title I have to be very careful with my answer. Don't you think so?"

"*I'm* not in a position to advise *you*," Halder said.

"Exactly," Mason conceded. "I appreciate your frankness, Counselor. And since you're not in a position to advise me I have to advise myself. Now then, you've raised a very interesting question. I don't know, under the circumstances, if I am at liberty to comment on any matter of title. However, go right ahead with your interrogation and I'll see what can be done."

Halder looked back at his paper. "While you were in that house," he said, "the house belonging to Ed Davenport at Paradise, didn't you pick the lock on a desk, open a lockbox, and remove an envelope on which there was written in Davenport's handwriting 'To be delivered to the authorities in the event of my death'?"

Mason paused thoughtfully.

"Can't you answer that question?" Halder asked.

Mason pursed his lips. "There are a good many factors involved in that question. I am trying to divide them in my own mind."

"Such as what?"

"In the first place," Mason said, "once more you bring in the question of the ownership of the house."

"Well, we can have it understood," Halder said, "that whenever I refer to the house as Ed Davenport's house I am talking about it in the general popular sense of the word and we won't try to adjudicate the title here and now.''

"Oh no," Mason said, "that would be an oral stipulation that I was not to be bound by my own statements. That might be all right as between you and me, Counselor, but it might not be all right as between some—well, let us say some cold-blooded, calculating, merciless attorney who might be representing some other heir to the estate.''

"What other heir?''

"Well," Mason said, "I haven't figured it all out yet, but for instance there's Sara Ansel. Sara Ansel's sister married William Delano's brother. Now let us suppose, for the sake of the argument, that the Delano estate could not come to Myrna Davenport.''

"Why not?''

"Oh because of various legal reasons, such, for instance, as the question—and, mind you, this is only a hypothetical question—that Myrna Davenport should be accused of the murder of William Delano.''

"She can't be," Halder said. "She's accused of the murder of Hortense Paxton, but Delano wasn't murdered. He was dying.''

"Then I have your assurance that she is not to be charged with the murder of William Delano? And I have your assurance William Delano was not murdered?''

"I'm not in a position to assure you of anything.''

"There we are," Mason said. "Right back to where we started. I find myself in a very peculiar position, Counselor. I am exceedingly anxious to co-operate with you but—''

"What are you getting at? That Sara Ansel might be an heir to the estate?''

"Well," Mason said, "suppose that Myrna was incapable of inheriting from William Delano under the will Delano left because of the fact that she was accused of murdering him. That would leave Mrs. Ansel perhaps in a position to inherit property which came to the dead brother of Delano—or would it? I'm frank to admit, Counselor, I haven't looked up the law of succession.''

"Neither have I," Halder said.

"Well, perhaps we'd better look it up now," Mason said.

"No, no," Halder said. "We're getting this thing in an interminable mess. I want to keep my questions simple and I'd like to have simple, definite answers."

"I'm certainly anxious to do it that way," Mason said, "but the fact that this has become a formal hearing complicates the situation enormously."

"I'm trying to make it informal."

"But you said it was formal."

"Well, that depends on what you call formal."

"Reading from a written list."

"Well, I tried to co-ordinate my thoughts in advance."

Mason looked at him reproachfully. "And that was the only reason for preparing the list, Counselor? The *only* reason?"

"Well, of course," Halder said, suddenly embarrassed, "I had conferred with other officials who suggested specific questions they wanted answered."

"And because you adopted their suggestions as to the questions that were to be answered you wrote them down?"

"In a way."

"There you are," Mason said. "This question that you have now asked me may have been thought up by the district attorney of Los Angeles County purely in an attempt to elaborate on some theory of the case that he has. And he may construe my answer in the most technical manner possible."

"But your client isn't charged with the murder of William Delano, her uncle. She's charged with the murder of Hortense Paxton."

"And that alleged murder enabled her to get most of the estate of William Delano?"

"That's my understanding of the situation."

"And the body of William Delano hasn't been exhumed?"

"No."

"Why not?"

"Because his was a natural death."

"How do you know?"

"The man was dying. He had been dying for months."

"Is a dying man immune to poison?"

"Are you trying to insinuate that your client poisoned William Delano?"

"Good heavens, no," Mason said. "*I* know she didn't."

"How do you know?"

"Because I know she didn't poison anyone."

"She poisoned Hortense Paxton," Halder said, "and she may have poisoned Edward Davenport."

"Oh, come, come," Mason said. "You're making a flat accusation."

"Well, I have information, Mr. Mason, which supports that accusation."

"Information which I don't have?"

"Certainly."

Mason said, "That, of course, complicates the situation again."

Halder said with exasperation, "I'm asking you simple questions and you go playing ring-around-a-rosy."

"It's not ring-around-a-rosy," Mason said. "I'm asking you to put yourself in my place. Would you answer questions involving the title to property?"

"I can't put myself in your place. I can't advise you. I have my own problems to worry about."

"Exactly," Mason said. "So, since I can't rely on your advice, since you're afraid to take the responsibility—"

"Who's afraid?" Halder demanded.

"Why, you are," Mason said.

"I'm not afraid of anything," Halder said, his face flushing, "and I'm not certain I like your attitude."

"Come, come," Mason said affably. "Let's not let the difference in our *official* positions enter into our *personal* relations, Counselor. I merely commented that you in your position were afraid to take the responsibility of advising me—"

"I'm not afraid to take the responsibility."

"Are you willing to advise me, then?"

"Certainly not. It's not my place to advise you. I'm representing the people of the State of California. I'm representing this county. You're representing a client. You'll have to decide what your own responsibilities are.''

Mason said, ''Of course, Counselor, it seems to me that by that answer you're evading the question.''

''*I'm* evading the question?'' Halder shouted.

''Precisely,'' Mason said. ''You won't answer definitely whether or not in my position as an attorney representing Myrna Davenport I should answer your questions.''

''I'm not in a position to advise you on anything.''

''Well,'' Mason said, his face suddenly breaking into a smile as though he had a complete solution, ''will you then assure me that if I go ahead and discuss questions of title with you my answers will not at any time be binding upon my client in regard to such matters?''

Halder hesitated and said, ''Why, I think—I don't see how they could.''

''But will you definitely assure me?'' Mason asked. ''Will you take the responsibility? Will you guarantee it?''

''Certainly not.''

''There you are,'' Mason said.

The lawyer settled back in his chair and smoked thoughtfully as though making a good-faith attempt at finding some way out of the impasse.

Halder glanced at the sheriff, then at his deputy. Abruptly he said, ''Mr. Mason, will you and Miss Street pardon us for a few minutes? You wait right here. I want to confer with my associates. Will you, Sheriff, and you, Oscar, mind stepping in this other office with me?''

The three scraped back their chairs, crowded through the door into the second office.

Della Street turned to Perry Mason. ''Well,'' she said, ''you seem to—''

Mason placed a warning finger to his lips and rolled his eyes around the room, then interrupted to say, ''I seem to be in a devil of a fix, don't I, Della? I'd like to be fair with Mr. Halder and I'd like to be frank. But for the life of me I don't see how I can overlook the fact that I'm in a position of responsibility as far as my client is concerned. Now you take that question of title and it could become very complicated.''

"Yes," Della Street said, "even with these few preliminary questions I can see that it's going to be complicated, and the district attorney has a list of several typewritten pages."

"Well," Mason said, "of course I want to co-operate with him, Della, but we have other things to do. We can't stay here indefinitely. I do hope he'll expedite matters."

Della Street smiled.

Mason winked at her. "Care for a cigarette, Della?"

"No, Chief, thank you."

Mason settled back to smoking. After a moment, he said, "I do hope they won't take too much time with their conference. After all, Della, we're holding a chartered plane here and I have very definite responsibilities back in my own office."

After a moment, Mason again winked at Della Street and said, "That's right, Della. Put your head back and try and get some sleep. After all, you've had quite a siege of it, being up all last night."

"Did I have my eyes closed?" Della Street asked innocently.

"Yes," Mason said. "If you can doze off by all means do so."

And Mason, with a finger on his lips, gestured for silence.

"Well, thanks," Della Street said, yawning audibly.

There was an interval of several minutes during which there was complete silence in the room. Della Street held her head against the back of the chair, her eyes closed. Mason smoked thoughtfully, from time to time holding his cigarette out in front of him, studying the eddying smoke.

At length the door from the other room opened. The three men filed back into the room. They were followed by a fourth.

Mason looked at the man and said, "Well, well, Sidney Boom. How are you, Mr. Boom? It's good to see you again."

He got up and shook hands.

Boom smiled. "How are you, Mr. Mason? How do you do, Miss Street?"

Della Street gave the officer her hand. "Nice to see you again."

"Thank you."

Chairs scraped once more.

Halder seemed to have decided upon a new line of attack. He turned to question Boom.

"You're an officer up at Paradise?"

"Yes."

"A deputy, working out of the sheriff's office here?"

"Yes, sir."

"And you were such a deputy last night?"

"Yes, sir."

"Now were you called to the residence of Ed Davenport last night?"

"That's the place out on Crestview Drive?"

"Don't ask me where it is. I asked you a question."

"Well, I'm not sure who owns the house except—yes, I am, too. The woman told me."

"What woman?" Mason asked.

"The secretary, Mabel Norge."

"Now just a moment," Mason said. "I can't sit here without registering some protest at this method of proving title."

"I'm not proving title," Halder said angrily. "I'm simply trying to confront you with some of the proof that *we* have."

"But you distinctly asked him about who owned the property," Mason said, "and he told you that the only way he knew was from a statement made by Mabel Norge. Now I submit that Mabel Norge isn't an expert on real estate titles and therefore any statement she made to him was simply hearsay and—"

"All right, all right," Halder said. "This isn't a court of law. We're not trying title to the property."

"But you raised the question of title."

"I'm merely describing the house."

"Then why not describe it with reference to the number of the location on Crestview Drive?"

"All right," Halder said. "Let's go at it this way, Boom. You were called out to a place on Crestview Drive. Where is it?"

"As you go out on Crestview Drive and come to the end

of the street it's the last place on the right—a big, rambling house surrounded by fruit and shade trees."

"You make a difference in your own mind between a fruit tree and a shade tree?" Mason asked.

"I do," Boom said.

"Well, now actually, Mr. Boom, a fruit tree can well give shade. You take these fig trees, I suppose one would call them fruit trees, and—"

"Now just a moment," Halder interpolated, his voice edged with anger. "I'm conducting the inquiry, Mr. Mason. I'm interrogating Mr. Boom at the moment, and I'm going to ask you to keep quiet."

"Regardless of any inaccuracies in Mr. Boom's statement?"

"Regardless of anything," Halder said. "I'm going to ask you to keep quiet."

"Very well," Mason said. "I trust that everyone here understands that I have been asked to keep quiet regardless of any inaccuracies in Mr. Boom's statements. I'm sorry, Counselor. I won't interrupt again. Go right ahead."

"You went out to this house?" Halder asked.

"I did."

"At whose request?"

"Mabel Norge."

"Who's she?"

"I understand she's the secretary for Ed Davenport. I've seen her around Paradise some."

"Did you know Davenport in his lifetime?"

"Yes, I've talked with him a few times."

"And you went out to this house at the request of Mabel Norge?"

"That's right. She was calling for the police."

"And what did you find?"

"I found the door unlocked, the lights on, and Mr. Mason and Miss Street making themselves very much at home."

"What else?"

"I was instructed by Mabel Norge to find a letter that had been written by Mr. Davenport and left with her with the

84

instructions that it was to be opened in the event of his death.''

''And what did you do?''

''I found that letter—that is, I found a lockbox which contained an envelope which was sealed. On the envelope there was a statement in Mr. Davenport's handwriting that it was to be delivered to the officers in the event of his death.''

''And what did you do with that?''

''I took it into my custody.''

''You have that envelope here?''

''You have it.''

''Well, you gave it to me, didn't you?''

''That's right.''

''And I have it here in my desk. You'd know that envelope if you saw it?''

''Certainly.''

''How would you know it?''

''Because I wrote my name on it.''

''And the date?''

''And the date.''

''And then what did you do with it?''

''I gave it to you.''

''We had some discussion about what should be done with the letter, didn't we?''

''That's right.''

''And I put it in the safe?''

''I believe so. You told me you put it in the safe.''

''And then this morning we got together again?''

''That's right.''

''And decided we'd better see what was in the letter?''

''That's right.''

''And we cut it open?''

''Yes.''

''And there was nothing in it except several sheets of blank paper?''

''That's right.''

''So then we started examining the envelope and decided it looked as though it might have been tampered with?''

''Yes, sir.''

"So we called in a man who is an expert in such matters and he told us that the gum arabic, or whatever it was that had originally been placed on the flap of the envelope with which to seal it, had been pretty well removed by being moistened and that the envelope had been steamed open and then sealed with mucilage and that this had probably been done within the last twenty-four hours?"

"That's right."

"All right," Halder said, turning to Mason, "what have you to say about that?"

"I'd say that you asked the questions very rapidly," Mason said, "and that Boom answered them without the least hesitancy."

"No, no, that's not what I mean. I mean what have you to say about the accuracy of his statements?"

"Oh, good heavens," Mason said. "You've taken me entirely by surprise. You specifically told me that I wasn't to say anything when his statements were inaccurate."

"I meant I didn't want you to interrupt."

"That wasn't the way you expressed it, I'm sure. You told me particularly to keep quiet."

"Well, I'm asking you to talk now."

"In what way?"

"I'm asking you to comment on Boom's statements."

"I'm quite certain they're not correct," Mason said. "Now wait a minute, Mr. Boom, don't get angry. I think that you *feel* they're correct, but I don't think that they are correct."

"In what respect are they wrong?" Halder asked.

"Oh, in many respects. For instance, I believe you said Davenport had written on the envelope in his handwriting that in the event of his death it was to be turned over to the officers."

"That's right."

Mason turned to Boom. "You'd seen Davenport in his lifetime?"

"That's right."

"You didn't know he was dead?"

"I don't *know* he's dead even now. I've been told he's dead."

"Now," Mason said, smiling, "you're answering the questions the way I think you should, Mr. Boom. You're confining your statements to your own knowledge. Now you stated that that was Mr. Davenport's handwriting on the envelope. You don't know whether that was Davenport's handwriting, do you?"

"Mabel Norge told me it was."

"I know, I know," Mason said. "That's hearsay. You don't *know* that it was in Davenport's handwriting."

"Certainly not."

"Now just a moment," Halder said. "I didn't bring Boom in here to be cross-examined."

Mason became angry for the first time. "What are you trying to do to me?" he asked "Are you trying to jockey me into a position where I can be misquoted?"

Halder jumped up from the chair. "What are you insinuating?" he demanded.

Mason said, "I'm not insinuating. I'm asking. First you tell me not to say anything if Boom's statements are incorrect. Then you challenge me to point out where they're incorrect. I start asking Boom questions in order to show by Boom's own statements where his answers are incorrect and you jump up and charge that I have no right to cross-examine Boom."

"Well, you haven't."

"I'm not cross-examining him."

"Well, it sounded like it to me."

"I'm simply trying to do what you told me to, to point out where his statements are incorrect."

"Well, that's what I call cross-examining. Point out someplace where he's made a wrong statement. I defy you to show anyplace where he has stated anything that isn't true."

"Why, there were lots of places," Mason said.

"Name one," Halder challenged.

"For instance," Mason said, "you have said a couple of times that the envelope contained the endorsement in Davenport's handwriting that in the event of his death it was to be turned over to the officers."

"Well, I've explained now that I only know it was his

handwriting because of what Mabel Norge told me,'' Boom said.

"So you don't know it's his handwriting?''

"I don't know it, no,'' Boom shouted.

"Well then,'' Mason said, "how do you know that the envelope contained the endorsement that it was to be turned over to the officers in the event of his death?''

"I saw it,'' Boom yelled. "I saw that with my own eyes.''

"Now just a minute,'' Mason said, "don't let your anger run away with you, Boom. You're a nice, observing officer. You don't mean that.''

"I mean every word of it.''

"That wasn't what was on the envelope,'' Mason said.

"Well, that's the effect of it. And I remember that's what Mabel Norge told me was on the envelope.''

"Exactly,'' Mason said. "Now if the district attorney will kindly show you the envelope, Mr. Boom, you'll find that that isn't what was on the envelope at all. The only words on the envelope are 'To be opened in the event of my death and the contents delivered to the authorities' and that is followed by what purports to be the signature of Ed Davenport.''

"Well, isn't that the same thing?'' Halder asked.

"Certainly not,'' Mason retorted. "In the one instance the instructions would have been that the envelope had been left in a sort of escrow to be delivered to the authorities unopened. But under the instructions actually written on the back of the envelope Mr. Davenport instructed his legal representatives—provided, of course, the words were in his handwriting—first to open the envelope and then, and only then, to deliver the contents to the authorities.''

There was a complete, sickening silence in the office.

"So you see,'' Mason said, beaming at Boom, "Mabel Norge described a different envelope. So it wasn't the pages *inside* of the envelope that had been substituted but it must have been the whole envelope. The envelope containing the message that Mabel Norge described to you couldn't be found. The envelope which she produced was an entirely different envelope from what she said it was because it had a different message.''

"Now wait a minute," Halder said. "That's the sheerest nonsense. You're trying to confuse the issues."

Mason said, "Sir, I consider that as an insult. I am simply trying to clarify the issues. I defy you to analyze any one of my statements here and find anything in it which tends to confuse any issue. I came up here in a spirit of co-operation. I could have told you to go to the devil. I could have told you to get a subpoena or issue a warrant, or try to make me appear before a grand jury—and if I had appeared before the grand jury I could have insisted upon your questions being technically accurate.

"As it is, I have chartered an airplane at great expense to myself. I have closed up my office for a day at a time when the most urgent demands were being made for my services. I have explained my position to you. I have asked you to put yourself in my position and to advise me if I should do anything different.

"You yourself, as an attorney, don't dare to advise me to do anything different, and now you're accusing me of confusing the issues. I don't like it. I—dammit, sir, you may consider my co-operation withdrawn. I have nothing further to state."

"You're going to have a lot more to state," Halder said. "You're in my county now. You aren't going to leave it without my permission."

"What do you mean by that?"

"I mean I can slap a subpoena on you. I can . . . I can arrest you."

"For what?"

"For being an accessory before . . . after the fact."

"Accessory to what?"

"Murder."

"Whose murder?"

"Ed Davenport's murder."

"Which is it," Mason asked, "an accessory before or an accessory after the fact?"

"I don't know. I—yes, I do, too. It's after the fact."

"What are the elements of murder?" Mason asked.

"You know them as well as I do."

"You'd better prove them then," Mason said. "One of the first elements of murder is a killing, a homicide, a dead body."

"Well, we haven't found the body yet but we're going to."

"The hell you are," Mason said. "Why don't you wake up?"

"Wake up to what?"

"Wake up to a consideration of the probabilities that Ed Davenport jumped out of the cabin window and ran away with his good-looking secretary, Mabel Norge. Where's Mabel Norge? Get her. Bring her here. She's charged me with tampering with an envelope. Let her make that accusation to my face."

"I . . . I haven't been able to locate Miss Norge as yet."

"Your 'as yet' is going to be a long time," Mason said.

"She's been very much upset by what has happened."

"I dare say she has," Mason said angrily. "I'm an attorney at law. I'm not going to sit here and be charged by Mabel Norge with having committed some crime. I demand that Mabel Norge be produced and confront me with her accusation. I want to question her in regard to it."

"I'm questioning you, that is I'm trying to."

"You're hurling accusations at me," Mason said, "made by Mr. Boom and Mabel Norge, and you won't confront me with my accusers."

"Mr. Boom is here."

"His accusations are hearsay."

"Some of them aren't."

"They all are," Mason said. He whirled to Boom. "What did Mabel Norge tell you about her reason for being at the house at that hour of the night?"

"She said she was driving by."

"You know that couldn't have been the truth," Mason said. "There was no place she could drive to."

"She could have made a circle in the driveway and gone out."

"Sure," Mason said. "That wouldn't have been driving by. The road ends there. She didn't say she went down to the house to see if things were all right. She said she was driving by casually, and then when I questioned her on that she admitted that was a false statement, didn't she?''

"Well—I'm not certain but what she did."

"And she didn't tell you about having been out there earlier that evening, did she?''

"Well, she worked there. I suppose—"

"About having been out there about thirty minutes before I arrived.''

"Thirty minutes before you arrived! Was she out there then?'' Boom asked.

"She didn't tell you about that?'' Mason asked.

"No."

"She didn't tell you about opening the desk and taking out that lockbox containing the envelope and substituting another envelope?''

"No, of course not. You were there. You heard the conversation."

"She drove away with you," Mason said. "She didn't tell you about that?''

"No."

"And she didn't tell you about going to the bank that afternoon and drawing out virtually every cent in the account of Ed Davenport with a check which he had previously given her, which was signed in blank, and which was intended to be used under those circumstances?''

Boom blurted, "She didn't *tell* me about that. I found out afterward at the bank—"

"Well, there you are," Mason said angrily, turning to Halder. "Why the devil don't you get the people in your own county? Why don't you clear this thing up without letting some district attorney down in Fresno, or some Los Angeles district attorney, try to tell you a murder has been committed and make a sucker out of you?

"Why don't you get hold of the parties here and really clean this thing up and air the facts instead of calling on an attorney from Los Angeles to come up here at considerable inconvenience to himself to answer a lot of accusations made by a woman who has resorted to flight?''

Halder said to Mason, "How the devil did *you* find out

about that withdrawal from the bank and the fact that Mabel Norge was missing?''

"Why?" Mason asked. "Wasn't I supposed to know it?"

"No one knows it. That's been a closely guarded secret. I told my office not to let it out to anyone."

"Good heavens," Mason said, "I should think it would have been obvious right from the start. Follow the pattern of the whole business."

"In that case—then you're claiming—that is, it's your position there wasn't any murder?"

"Murder?" Mason said. "Who the devil said there *was* a murder?"

"The doctor said the man was dead."

"And the witness said the corpse climbed out of a window."

Halder bit at his lip.

"Now then, let's get this straight," Mason said. "You were trying to conceal this information from me?"

"I wasn't making it public."

"You tried to keep me from finding out about it?"

"Well, if you want to put it that way, yes."

"I think under the circumstances," Mason said, "that I've been here now for some time endeavoring to co-operate with you, I think officially I have nothing further to say. I've answered your questions as freely and frankly as I can. I've given you something like an hour here."

"It hasn't been that long."

"Well, it's been quite awhile," Mason said. "Long enough for you to have covered the situation pretty thoroughly. I'm going to start back to my office."

"You can't leave this county until I tell you you can."

"The hell I can't. Try to stop me."

"I've got lots of ways of stopping you."

"Try any one of them," Mason said, "and by tomorrow morning your face will be just as red as a boiled lobster."

Perry Mason nodded to Della Street and strode out of the office, leaving a somewhat dazed group of men moving into a quick, huddled conference.

Newsmen clustered around Mason as he came out.

"Well?" they asked. "What happened?"

Mason carefully closed the door, smiled and said, "I believe, boys, the district attorney told you that he'd issue a statement following the interview in which he'd give you all the news. If you'll go in and interview him I think he'll be glad to answer questions, and, under the circumstances, I'd prefer to have him do so."

Mason caught the eye of the reporter from *The Oroville Mercury* and winked at him.

The other reporters opened the door and tumbled into the inner office.

Pete Ingram joined Mason. "Okay?" he asked.

"Get us in your car and out to the airport fast," Mason said. "I'll talk on the way out."

"This way," Ingram said.

They hurried out of the sheriff's office. Ingram's car was at the curb.

"Make it snappy," Mason told him.

"What happened?" Ingram asked, putting the car into gear.

Mason said, "It was quite an interview. What do you have on it?"

"About all we have is that the interview took some time, that we could hear the rumble of voices which toward the last began to be raised in anger. Apparently the interview started harmoniously but ended on a sour note."

Mason said, "The interview was recorded on tape. Why don't you insist that—?"

"Not a chance. He wouldn't even admit that it was recorded."

"Well," Mason said, "let me drive the car. You ask questions and take notes and I'll answer questions, because the minute we get to the airport we're taking off."

The reporter stopped the car, opened the door, and ran around to get in on the other side. Mason slid across under the wheel.

"All right," he said, "start asking questions."

"What happened?" Ingram asked.

"To begin with," Mason said, "the district attorney said

it was going to be a formal interview, so it was conducted on that basis. Every time he asked a question, for instance, referring to the house in Paradise as Ed Davenport's house, I argued the question of title.''

"On what basis?"

Mason outlined the point under discussion and then went on while he was driving to the airport to give Ingram a fair summary of the interview.

At the airport Mason and Della Street disembarked from the car and went over to where the aviator was listening to a radio.

"Okay," Mason said. "Let's put this show on the road."

"Right away," the aviator said. "Say, did you folks hear the news broadcast that just came in?"

"What about it?" Mason asked.

"You're interested in that case down in Fresno," the aviator said. "They've found the body."

"Whose body?"

"This man Davenport whose wife killed him."

"Where was the body?"

"Buried in a shallow grave just two or three miles out of Crampton. At least they think it's Davenport's body. It was clad in pajamas with red dots or figures. It was just discovered a few minutes ago. They're still digging at the grave. A news service put it on the air."

Mason glanced at Ingram. Ingram grinned.

Mason said to the aviator, "Get that plane warmed up and get it warmed up fast. Taxi down the field just as soon as you can get under way. Warm up your motors at the far end of the field and then take off. No matter who tries to stop you, take off. Come on. Let's go. There's a hundred extra for you if you take off before anyone stops us."

They climbed aboard the plane. The aviator started the motors and after a few seconds moved slowly down to the far end of the field where he swung the plane around and warmed up the motors.

Mason leaned forward and said over the roar of the engines, "How are you coming? Ready to take off?"

"Just a few seconds now."

Mason said, "There's a car turning in. I want to get off before it arrives. I don't want any more delay."

"Oh, he's just stopping there to—"

"He isn't stopping," Mason said.

"Neither am I," the pilot said, gunning the motors.

The plane started down the field.

The car swung so that its lights cut across the path of the plane. A blood-red spotlight blazed into brilliance and a siren screamed its warning.

The pilot grinned as he gently picked the wheels off the ground.

"These motors make such an awful racket," he said, "that it's hard to hear a thing when you're taking off. For a minute I almost thought I heard a siren."

"I didn't hear a thing," Mason told him.

"Back to Sacramento?" the pilot asked.

"Not Sacramento," Mason said. "Fresno. And if you can drop me in there without filing a flight plan so that no one knows just where we're landing, it'll suit me fine."

"You don't want to stop at Sacramento?"

"Go right over Sacramento," Mason said, "just as high as you can get this crate into the air."

Chapter 7

The plane approached the lighted area which marked the location of Fresno.

"You can go on to Los Angeles?" Mason asked the pilot.

"Sure. I have to get gasoline, that's all."

Mason said, "Land at Fresno just as though you were making a routine stop for gasoline. I'll get out. You fill up with gas and take Miss Street on into Los Angeles."

"How about you?"

"I'll stop off here."

"Okay by me."

"When you get to Los Angeles," Mason said, "I'd just as soon you didn't talk with a lot of newspaper people. If you can land and manage to keep from being interviewed I'll appreciate it. Miss Street will settle up with you by check just before you land. Okay?"

"Okay."

Mason said to Della Street, "I'll be in touch with you, Della. Try and get some sleep if you can."

"How about Paul?"

"I'll get in touch with him from here."

She slipped her hand in his. He squeezed it gently. "Good girl," he said.

"When will you be in?"

"Tomorrow morning perhaps. There's work to do here."

"How much?"

"I don't know."

"Better fasten your seat belts," the pilot said. "We're coming in."

He swung in a wide circle and landed at the airport. As soon as he had taxied up and stopped the motor Mason jumped out, hurried into the administration building and into a telephone booth, where he hunched over with his right hand at his head so that his face wasn't visible from the outside.

Mason put through a collect call to Drake's office and within a few minutes had Paul Drake on the line.

"What are you doing up there in Fresno?" Drake asked.

"Looking around."

"Have they caught you?"

"Who?"

"The Fresno authorities."

"No."

"They're looking for you."

"On what grounds?" Mason asked.

"The authorities think you slipped over a fast one."

"How come?"

"That letter that Davenport left to be opened at the time of his death."

"What about it?"

"They think you have the original sheets that were in there and that you stuffed it with six sheets of blank paper."

"And what does that make me?" Mason asked.

"According to the district attorney up there it may make you an accessory after the fact."

"Go on," Mason told him. "What's next? Where's Mrs. Davenport?"

"Apparently she's in Fresno."

"I understand they found the body."

"That's right."

"No question of identification?"

"None whatever. It was buried in a shallow grave. Now here's a funny one, Perry. The grave had been dug for two or three days. It was all in readiness."

"You're sure?"

"That's right."

"How do they know?"

"Some kids had found it and had been playing around in it, using it for a fort. That's how they happened to find the body so easily. The kids reported that somebody had filled up their fort. Then they went ahead and described it to their parents—an oblong hole that had been filled in. The father of one of the kids went out to take a look. He became curious. The soil was easy to dig. He dug down two or three feet and struck the foot of a corpse. He went back and got the authorities and they uncovered Ed Davenport.''

"How long had he been dead?"

"Since yesterday. Apparently Dr. Renault had the right idea and the authorities are now busily engaged in begging his pardon.''

"What about the man who saw the corpse climb out the window?"

"Police are acting on the theory a male accomplice loaded the body into a car, then climbed out the window.''

"Wearing pajamas?"

"They think so—as a blind just in case anyone saw him.''

"What else?"

"You had the right hunch on the alias. I think we're ahead of the cops on that. Frank L. Stanton was registered at Welchburg's Motel there in Fresno. Evidently it was Davenport all right. The description fits him and he even gave the right license number on his automobile, but he wasn't drinking. He had someone visit him and there was a conference rather late at night. One of the couples in an adjoining cabin complained.''

"Man or woman?"

"Who?"

"In the conference.''

"A man. We don't know too much about it. We talked casually with Mrs. Welchburg but not enough to alarm her. We were afraid she might go to the police if we asked too many questions, and you might not like that.''

"I wouldn't,'' Mason said.

"Okay,'' Drake told him. "You're up there. It's all yours. Here's another one, Perry. Your friend Sara Ansel has been haunting the office. Gertie, at the switchboard, told her she might leave any message with me, that I might be in touch with you.''

"What does she want?'' Mason asked.

"She's now very contrite. She's had a complete change of heart. She says she acted on impulse when she lost faith in

Myrna Davenport. She was tired and her suspicious nature got the better of her. She now says she wishes she could cut her tongue out.''

"But before she had this change of heart she told everything she knew to the police?'' Mason asked.

"Oh definitely. She blabbed everything. Then the police got a little rough with her and made her mad. So she got to thinking things over and decided she had condemned Myrna Davenport on circumstantial evidence without a hearing. Now she's tearful and repentant. She wants you to know that you can depend on her and she wants to get word to Myrna through you.''

"How nice,'' Mason said.

"Isn't it? She blabs everything she knows and then comes running back for forgiveness—or perhaps to get another earful to peddle.''

"You think the police sent her?'' Mason asked.

"Could be,'' Drake said, "but it's a good act if it's an act. Those are genuine tears she's shedding all right. She wants you to call her just as soon as I get in touch with you. She left a number. Do you want it?''

"Hell, no,'' Mason said. "I'd call her long-distance from here and within five minutes she'd report to the police that I was in Fresno and I'd have every officer in the country on my trail.''

"That's the way I figured it. What are you going to do now?''

"Go to the Welchburg Motel, get a room, and try and get some information out of Mrs. Welchburg.''

"Going to register under an assumed name?''

"No,'' Mason said. "That would be flight. I'm going to register under my own name and I'll probably have twenty minutes to half an hour before the officers pick me up. How long had that grave been dug, Paul?''

"Three days at least. The kids had been playing in it for three days before Davenport's death.''

"That's going to make it bad,'' Mason said. "The D.A. will use that as evidence of premeditation.''

"He's done that already in an interview given to the press.

He calls it one of the most dastardly, cold-blooded, premeditated murders he has ever encountered."

"Okay," Mason said. "I'll be seeing you."

Mason remained in the telephone booth until he felt certain he was not observed, then slipped out to call a taxicab and went at once to the Welchburg Motel.

The woman who sat behind the desk in the office was somewhere in her fifties, a rather matronly figure with a kind mouth but with sharp, peering eyes.

"Hello," Mason said. "I'm here without any baggage. Didn't expect to stay. All I have is money."

"That's all we want," Mrs. Welchburg told him. "We have two units left. You can take your choice at five dollars."

Mason handed her the five dollars and at the same time gave her one of his cards. "I'm a lawyer," he said. "I'm trying to find out something about a case up here."

"Indeed."

"I wanted to find out about a Frank L. Stanton," Mason said. "He was here a couple of nights ago."

"Oh yes. Why, you're the *second* person who's been asking about him."

Mason smiled affably and said, "Mr. Stanton has quite a few interests."

"What's the matter? Did he do something? Did he—?"

"Not as far as I know," Mason said. "It's simply a question of serving some papers on him."

"Oh!" she said sharply, and then after a moment, her eyes suspicious, asked, "Divorce?"

Mason shook his head. "I'm not free to go into the details but it has to do with an option on a piece of mining property. The option time will be up within a couple of days, and in the event the purchaser should want to take up the option— well, you can see it would be rather embarrassing if Mr. Stanton couldn't be found."

"Oh yes, I see. Well, he was only here for one night. He left his address in Los Angeles."

"I have his address," Mason said, "but he isn't home and—well, there are still a couple of days to run, but it would be very embarrassing if he should try to conceal himself. Do you remember much about him?''

''Not very much,'' she said. ''He was in the mining business, I know that. He carried two suitcases with him, rather heavy suitcases, and he said something about having some samples in them.''

''Of ore?''

''I guess so. He had a new handbag he'd bought.''

''New?'' Mason asked.

''That's right. It was wrapped up, that is, covered with paper except for the handle, and I know from the way he picked it up it was empty, but the suitcases certainly were full.''

''Two of them?''

''That's right.''

''Well, I wonder if anyone was with him or whether he was alone?''

''No, he was alone. That's the only thing that I definitely remember. He had some visitors. About eleven-thirty a call came in from a man who had the adjoining unit. He said that he didn't like to complain but the people in the place I'd rented to Mr. Stanton were talking and it was keeping him awake. He asked if I'd mind giving that unit a ring and asking them to be more quiet.''

''Loud talk? An argument?'' Mason asked.

''Apparently not. Apparently it was just the opposite. They were talking in low voices but they were talking and it was rather late. You know how those things are when you're trying to sleep and some little monotonous noise, the drip of a water faucet, or something like that, will magnify itself until you're terribly nervous.''

''I understand,'' Mason said. ''You wouldn't know anything about what time Mr. Stanton left here in the morning?''

''No, I don't. I am up sometimes until one or two or sometimes three o'clock in the morning, and I usually sleep late. The maids take care of the units.''

''You certainly have a nice place here.''

''Thank you.''

''How many units do you have?''

"Fifty-two."

"Quite a place," Mason said. "Running it must be quite a job."

"It certainly is."

"I presume you have your problems."

"We certainly do."

"What did Mr. Stanton say when you rang his room and told him he was disturbing someone?"

"He said he was in a conference and that they were just finishing up. I guess that was true, too. I looked out of the door and saw there was a car parked in front of his unit. It was driven away just a few minutes later."

"You don't know what kind of a car?"

"No, it was just an average car. Just one of the popular makes. I wouldn't know which. I'm not much on spotting cars. My husband can take a look at a car and tell the year, the make and the model as far as he can see it. I'm not much good at it."

"Stanton didn't put in any long-distance telephone calls, did he?" Mason asked.

"As to that I couldn't say. You see, we can't very well bill things like that on the rooms. When people want to put through calls we prefer that they go to the pay stations in the lobby. We have two telephone booths there with pay telephones. Of course we *can* put through a long-distance call and have the person talk in his room. Sometimes we do that when we know the party, but with strangers we don't encourage it."

"And Mr. Stanton didn't ask for any long-distance service?"

"Not while I was here, and I'm certain he didn't get any because there wasn't any on the bill."

"But he could have gone to the booths in the lobby and put through a call?"

"Oh yes."

"And that wouldn't have been noticed?"

"No, not at all."

Mason said, "Well, I'll put through a call myself, I guess."

He was smiling cheerfully as he entered the telephone booth, dropped a coin, and asked to be connected with the sheriff's office. After the connection had been made he insisted on talking to the person in charge and when he had the undersheriff on the line, said, "I'm Perry Mason, an attorney. I came up here to consult with my client, Mrs. Edward Davenport. You have her incarcerated. I want to talk with her."

"You . . . you . . . you're Perry Mason?"

"That's right."

The voice suddenly became suave. "And where are you now, Mr. Mason?"

Mason said, "I'm at the Welchburg Motel and I'm going to get a taxi to come to your office. I want to talk with my client."

"Well, now, Mr. Mason, you don't need to bother at all," the voice said. "We try to be hospitable up here and we'll provide you with transportation. You stay right where you are and you'll have a car within five minutes."

"Within five minutes?"

"Well, maybe less," the voice told him. "Just a moment, please, I'll see what I can do. Hold the line."

There was some thirty seconds of silence, then the voice was back on the line. "We'll have a car there for you, Mr. Mason. We've been looking for you."

"Have you indeed?" Mason said.

"Yes. You went to Mr. Davenport's house in Paradise, didn't you?"

"No."

"You didn't?" the voice asked incredulously.

"No," Mason said. "I went to *Mrs.* Davenport's house, and in case you're interested in finding out about the contents of the envelope I suggest that you interrogate Mabel Norge, Mr. Davenport's secretary. Incidentally, in case you're interested any further, Mr. Davenport stayed here the night before his death, at the Welchburg Motel. He was registered under the name of Frank L. Stanton."

"You're sure?" the officer asked.

"The description fits, also the license number of the car."

"Why are you giving us that information?" the officer inquired.

"Good heavens!" Mason exclaimed in surprise. "Is there any reason why I shouldn't?"

"No, I guess not. We felt you might be just as happy if we didn't share your information."

"What gave you that idea? There's a car with a red light turning in the driveway. I suppose that's my transportation. You got it here pretty fast."

"We try to work fast, Mr. Mason," the undersheriff said. "It just happened we had a radio car cruising in your neighborhood and just oddly enough they were making a canvass of the various motels trying to find where Mr. Davenport had stayed."

"Well, I'm glad I saved you some trouble," Mason said, and hung up as two broad-shouldered deputy sheriffs pushed their way into the lobby.

Chapter 8

The police car pulled in to the curb and as Mason was escorted into the building, a tall man with a good-natured grin came forward and extended his hand.

"Perry Mason?"

"That's right," Mason said, taking the proffered hand.

"I'm Talbert Vandling," the man said. "I'm the district attorney here in Fresno. Looks as though I'm going to be trying a murder case with you on the other side."

Mason sized the man up. The cool, steady eyes, the easy, relaxed affability which emanated from him.

"I think," he said, "you might be rather a dangerous antagonist."

"I'd try to be," Vandling told him. "Now what's all this about you opening a letter up in Butte County?"

"Am I supposed to have opened a letter?" Mason asked.

"The D.A. up there thinks you did."

"Was it a crime?"

"Well," Vandling said, "that depends on how you look at it."

Mason smiled at him. "I take it you have troubles of your own down here in your county."

"You can say that again."

"Then I take it it won't be necessary for you to borrow any problems from Butte County in order to keep yourself comfortably busy."

Vandling threw back his head and laughed.

Mason said, "I understand you're holding Mrs. Edward Davenport here. She's my client. I want to talk with her and advise her as to her rights."

The smile left Vandling's face. "There are some things about that case I can't understand, Mason. Now I don't want to prosecute anyone who isn't guilty. According to her story she knows nothing about the murder. In other words, she's innocent.''

Mason nodded.

''Unfortunately,'' Vandling said, ''there are some circumstances which make it impossible for me to accept her story at face value.''

''How about the corpse climbing out of the window?'' Mason asked.

''That's one of the things I was coming to,'' Vandling said. ''I'm going to put my cards on the table and I'd like to have you put your cards on the table.''

''Well,'' Mason said, ''let's not do it all at once. You put down one of your cards and I'll see if I can match it.''

''All right,'' Vandling said. ''The police made an investigative blunder. I'll be perfectly frank in telling you that.''

''How come?''

''The man who saw the figure, apparently clad in pajamas, climb out of the window and drive away has slipped through our fingers.''

''How did that happen?''

''He gave a fictitious address and presumably a false name to the officers.''

''And the officers let it go at that?''

Vandling said, ''Figure it out for yourself. He was registered there at this motel. He wasn't alone. The couple was registered as husband and wife. He told the officers about having seen the figure in pajamas getting out of the window and driving away in the automobile. The officers asked for his name and address. He gave them the name and the address under which he was registered. The officers checked that. They found that he'd registered the night before under that name and they let it go at that. They didn't ask to see his driving license. They didn't check the number of his car. They didn't ask for any identification. It was a hell of a blunder. The only reason they were so lax was because at that time they felt certain there wasn't any corpse, that a man who had been locked in was making a getaway from an unattractive wife.''

Mason's eyes hardened. "Go on," he said.

"Evidently this man started doing a lot of second thinking. He realized that if he was going to be a witness his real identity and perhaps that of his companion would come out. So he got away from there fast."

"And the officers don't know who he is?"

"Haven't the faintest idea. They have the name that he gave them, but I'm pretty certain it isn't his right name. The address is fictitious and the license number of the automobile that he put on his motel registration was false."

"How do you know?"

"We've checked the owner of the automobile that's registered under that license. He's in the southern part of the state, he's married, has a family, and there's no question that he isn't the man we want. Moreover, he hasn't left his home in the past forty-eight hours and neither has his automobile. He hasn't loaned the car to anyone and it couldn't possibly have been up here in this part of the state."

Mason said, "That man in the motel has become the most valuable witness for the defense."

Vandling nodded.

"If that had been a witness whose story had been of value to the prosecution," Mason said, "I don't think he'd have slipped through the fingers of the police."

Vandling said, "Well, there are certain implications in what you say and in the way you say it that I don't like."

"There are certain implications in what has happened that I don't like."

Vandling's infectious smile came back. "Are you going to be hard to get along with?" he asked.

Mason's lips smiled at the man, but his eyes remained cold and hard. "Yes," he said.

"I was afraid of that," Vandling told him. "Of course, Mason, let's be fair about this. If the man had been a witness for the prosecution his statement would have indicated that a murder had been committed. Right?"

"I suppose so."

"So the officers would have known that they were working on a murder, that they'd be dragged over the coals if the witness slipped through their fingers and they'd naturally have taken steps to check his identity and make sure they had the means of locating him as a witness.

"But as it was, this man's story indicated that no crime had been committed. Therefore the officers were more careless than would have otherwise been the case—at least I hope they were. It was an investigative blunder and I don't like it. I don't feel easy about it at all."

"That was an important witness," Mason said. "The police should have seen that he was available."

"I agree with you."

"So where does that leave us now?" Mason asked.

"I'm afraid," Vandling said, "it leaves you and me in a position where we have a conflict of interests. The way things look now I'm going to have to put a murder charge against Myrna Davenport. I'm going to have to prosecute that charge. Naturally I don't want to do it if Ed Davenport actually did climb out of the window of that motor court.

"However, even if we found that witness, about all he could testify to was that he saw a figure, which he presumes was a masculine figure, clad in pajamas, getting out of the window, that he noticed the man was barefoot, that he got in an automobile and drove away. The figure matches the general description of Ed Davenport."

"You've found the body?" Mason asked.

"We've found the body."

"Any question but what it's Ed Davenport's body?"

"None whatever."

"How was the body dressed?" Mason asked.

"In pajamas. It was barefoot and it had been buried in a grave that had been dug two or three days in advance."

"You mean it was buried in a hole in the ground that had been there for some time?"

"Well, that's your way of presenting it," Vandling said. "As far as I'm concerned it was a grave that had been dug several days in advance and dug for the specific purpose of receiving Davenport's body."

"And how did he die?" Mason asked.

"We don't know that for sure," Vandling said, "but our best guess is that it was poison."

"Arsenic?"

"Potassium cyanide. We haven't had the autopsy yet."

"Then death would have been almost instantaneous."

Vandling nodded.

"The candy?" Mason asked.

"The candy in his bag was loaded with arsenic and potassium cyanide. Most of the pieces had arsenic. Some of them had potassium cyanide. It was a neat job of poisoning. Part of the liquid had been drained out, evidently with a suction needle, and liquid containing poison had been introduced."

"Why the devil would anyone have used two types of poison?" Mason asked.

Vandling said, "I'd like to have the answer to that, too."

"Particularly," Mason said, "a slow-acting poison and one that would have taken effect almost immediately."

"It's a question," Vandling admitted. "In fact, there are questions in this case that I can't answer. I don't like to prosecute a case unless I know that I have a case. If I ask a jury to return the death penalty against this woman, I want to be certain that she is guilty of cold-blooded, premeditated, first-degree murder."

Mason nodded.

"I've read a lot about you," Vandling went on. "You're a tough, resourceful fighter. You believe in the dramatic. I'm not too keen to go up against you in a case where I can't be sure it's dead open-and-shut."

"And so?" Mason asked.

Vandling's friendly smile was once more in evidence. "And so," he said, "that's all I can say to you *at the present time.*"

"What is?"

"I'll repeat. I don't like to ask for the death penalty in a case unless I'm sure it's cold-blooded, deliberate, premeditated murder; that there are some things in this case I can't explain at the present time. I don't seem to have the answers. There's a defense witness who has slipped through the fingers of the police.

"I have a reputation to maintain as a prosecutor. You're dynamite. You're deadly dangerous. If there are any facts in a case that the prosecution can't explain, you're going to dramatize those facts in some way so that they seem to be the most important facts in the entire case."

"And so?" Mason asked.

"That's all I can say *at the present time*."

"Well, let's look ahead a little."

"I'm not a fortune teller or a prophet."

"Let's explore some of the possibilities that *might* happen."

Vandling said, "If you put it on that basis, a prosecutor nearly always finds that when he has enough evidence to prove a person is guilty there are some elements in the case that he still can't account for. When that happens he sometimes goes ahead and gets a conviction anyway. Sometimes he offers to make a deal."

"What sort of a deal?"

"Oh, it runs into all kinds of things. Sometimes he agrees not to ask for the death penalty if the defendant pleads guilty. Sometimes he lets the defendant plead guilty to second-degree murder. Sometimes, in extreme cases, if the defendant can make a good showing, he's willing to accept a manslaughter plea."

"But in this particular case?" Mason asked.

"In this particular case," Vandling said, "I am not in a position to say anything further *at the present time*."

"Well, I guess we understand each other," Mason told him.

"And you want to see the defendant, I take it."

Mason nodded.

Vandling said, "I came down here personally because I wanted to meet you and because I wanted to assure you that you aren't going to have the slightest trouble seeing the defendant. Up in this county we don't go in for a lot of third-degree stuff. We don't try to keep a defendant away from counsel. You'll find Mrs. Davenport waiting for you in a conference room, and I'll give you my personal assurance that there aren't any bugs in that room. It isn't wired. Whatever you say to each other is going to be private and confidential. If Mrs. Davenport wants to talk to me I'll ask her questions from time to time. If she doesn't want to answer them that's her privilege. You're her attorney and you're going to have every professional courtesy extended to you in this county and we're going to safeguard the rights of the defendant just as jealously as you are.''

"Thanks," Mason said.

"And," Vandling went on, "if the evidence indicates that she deliberately poisoned her husband I'm going to ask for the death penalty.''

Mason nodded.

"And if she gets acquitted up here," Vandling said, "the district attorney in Los Angeles wants her, to charge her with the poison murder of Miss Hortense Paxton.''

Again Mason nodded.

"I thought you might like to know those things," Vandling said, "particularly in case you considered having the defendant plead guilty. Right now, in view of the fact that an important defense witness seems to have given the police the slip, if you wanted to go into court, comment on that fact and have your client plead guilty, I would certainly advise the court that under those circumstances the prosecution would be content to ask for life imprisonment and not for the death penalty.''

"And then they'd take her back to Los Angeles to try her for the murder of Hortense Paxton," Mason said, "and when she got on the stand to deny her guilt the district attorney would cross-examine her and by way of impeachment would say, 'Isn't it a fact that you have been convicted of a felony?' and she would have to say, 'Yes.' Then he would say, 'Isn't it a fact that you were convicted of poisoning your husband up in Fresno County?' and she'd have to say, 'Yes.' And then the jury in Los Angeles would decide she was a habitual poisoner and would close their ears to any evidence that might be in her favor, would find that she was guilty of the poison murder of Hortense Paxton and would sentence her to death.''

Vandling placed his hand to his face, rubbed his fingers along the angle of his jaw, and then slowly nodded. "Yes," he said at length, "I can see that you have your problems, too, Counselor."

"So," Mason said, "I'll go and talk with my client. Thanks for putting the cards on the table. I have an idea it's going to be rather tough trying a case with you on the other side."

Vandling's fingers gripped Mason's hand. "I'm going to try my damnedest to make it tough," he said. "How about what happened up in Paradise? How about that letter with the blank sheets of paper in it and the flap that had been steamed open? You want to make any statement about that?"

Mason shook his head.

"I didn't think you would," Vandling said. "The D.A. up there telephoned me that I'd find you loquacious but evasive. He said you'd talk your head off but wouldn't say anything."

Mason said, "A man's tactics change with different people and with different circumstances. I think it would be rather difficult to be loquacious and evasive with you."

"I'd try to make it so," Vandling said. "Well, go ahead and see your client, Mason, and anything we can do here to make you comfortable just call on us. I'm a Rotarian myself. I'd like to take you down to the club and introduce you. If you like to play golf, we can fix you up and—"

"Thanks," Mason said. "I'm afraid I'm going to be pretty busy."

"I'll sure *try* to keep you busy," Vandling told him. "Good luck. I think you're going to need it. Perhaps we both are."

Chapter 9

Mason found Mrs. Davenport waiting for him in a small, office-like room which contained comfortable chairs and a small table. Aside from the peculiarly stale atmosphere, permeated with the sweetish smell of disinfectant, there was nothing to indicate the environment of a jail.

Myrna Davenport looked quickly at Mason, then came toward him and put her hand in his. The fingers somehow seemed to cling to the lawyer's hand as though drawing strength from him.

"I'm so glad you came," she said in her characteristic low monotone. "They told me you were here. The district attorney is very nice."

"Did you talk with him?"

"Yes."

"What did you tell him?"

"As much as I knew of what had happened."

"Did you sign anything?"

"No."

Mason said, "From now on quit talking. Let the other people do the talking."

"What shall I say if they ask me questions?"

"Refer them to me. Say that I'm answering all questions."

"But, Mr. Mason, I'd like to get this thing cleared up. I'd like to—"

"Sure you'd like to get it cleared up," Mason said. "Who wouldn't? But when you get *this* cleared up they're going to drag you back to Los Angeles and try you for the murder of Hortense Paxton."

"Won't they do it anyway? Won't they—?"

Mason shook his head.

"Each county is hoping the other one will take the first

113

crack at you. If you get convicted of anything in either county you'll get the death penalty in the other. Let's be frank. Let's put the cards on the table and face the facts."

Myrna Davenport sat down abruptly in one of the chairs as though her knees had lost their strength.

"Does it hurt much?" she asked.

"What?" Mason asked.

"Death by gas."

Mason eyed her sharply. "They say it's completely painless. You take one whiff and pass out in a tenth of a second."

"Well," she said, "that's a relief. Someone told me they choked and strangled and coughed and suffered."

"Who told you that?"

"One of the people in here."

"One of the officers?"

"No. An inmate."

"A woman?"

"Yes."

Mason said, "Stay away from her. Don't talk with anybody. Don't form any friendships. Sit tight. Leave things in my hands."

"You're going to continue to represent me?" she asked.

Mason nodded.

"I was afraid you'd . . . afraid you might back out."

"I don't back out," Mason told her. "Even if you're guilty you're entitled to a fair trial. You're entitled to all of your rights under the law. It's my business to see that you get them."

"Thank you."

"Are you guilty?"

"No."

"Of poisoning Hortense Paxton?"

"No."

"Of poisoning your husband?"

"No."

"You've got some things to explain," Mason said wearily, drawing up a chair and sitting down across from her.

"I know."

114

Mason watched her sharply, ''Your friend, Sara Ansel turned against you.''

''She's back in my corner now.''

''How do you know?''

''She telephoned.''

''Did they let you take a telephone message?''

''From her, yes.''

Mason said angrily, ''They were monitoring the conversation. What did she say? Anything?''

''Only that she had doubted me and turned against me and had told the police everything she knew and a lot of things she didn't know, and then she started thinking things over and had become thoroughly ashamed of herself.''

Mason said, ''She had told police she watched you digging a hole and burying some poisons.''

Myrna Davenport's eyes raised to Mason's. For a moment there was a distinct flicker of panic in them.

''She told the police that?''

Mason nodded.

Myrna folded her hands on her lap, looked down at them, and said, ''Well, of course, she had every reason to doubt me.''

''You packed your husband's bags when he went on trips?''

''Oh yes.''

''He carried candy with him?''

''Yes, always.''

''You bought that candy?''

''Yes.''

''The candy in his bag was poisoned.''

''I know. They told me.''

''You didn't poison it?''

''No.''

''Who did?''

''I don't know.''

''You had been living in the house in Paradise?''

''Yes.''

''And after your uncle, William Delano, became ill, you went to live with him?''

''Yes.''

"And what did your husband do?"

"He stayed up in Paradise most of the time, but he would come and visit us."

"Your husband didn't like the idea of you moving down to Los Angeles?"

"No."

"Why?"

"He said that I was letting myself in for a lot of drudgery and making a nursemaid out of myself, that when Uncle William died I'd never get a dime out of the estate."

"What made him say that?"

"He thought it was all fixed for Hortense to get it all. Even after she died Ed didn't want me there. He didn't like Aunt Sara. For some reason Ed thought Aunt Sara would manage to get the bulk of the money some way."

"If you get convicted of murdering Hortense Paxton, she may do it yet," Mason said. "There's a peculiar legal question involved."

"I didn't murder Hortie. I loved her."

"Your husband never moved down to the house in Los Angeles, did he?"

"Not until after Uncle William died. After that he did. But, of course, he kept a lot of things up there in Paradise. He turned that into his office. It was easier to run his mining deals from up there."

"You packed his bags," Mason said. "Do you remember packing them when he left for Paradise the last time?"

"Yes."

"What did you pack?"

"Not many clothes because he kept most of his wardrobe in Paradise. I packed some shirts, socks, pajamas—"

"You remember the pajamas?"

"Yes."

"What were they?"

"White, with red figures."

"What sort of figures?"

"Something like a fleur-de-lis."

"Have you seen the pajamas he was wearing when the body was found?"

"No."

"They haven't shown those to you?"

"No."

"They haven't asked you to look at the body?"

"No."

"They probably will," Mason said. "You'll have to steel yourself for the shock."

"Yes, I know."

"Think you can do it?"

"Yes, of course."

"Why do you say of course?"

"I'm not very emotional."

"I'll say you aren't," Mason said angrily. "You can't seem to understand the predicament you're in."

"I understand it."

"Now when you packed up your husband's bag the last time he left, you put a box of candy in it?"

"Yes."

"Where did you get that candy?"

"I bought it at a candy store. I bought two boxes. I put one box in and left the other box in the bureau drawer."

"Did you open one of those boxes of candy?"

"No."

"You're certain?"

"Yes, of course."

"You didn't even tamper with the wrapping?"

"No. It was just the way it came from the candy store except for the outer paper. The box was wrapped in cellophane. I didn't cut the cellophane at all."

"Then you're certain they can't find any of your fingerprints on any of those candies?"

"Of course not."

"Someone opened the box and filled the candies with poison—two different kinds of poisons."

"So they tell me."

"That wasn't you?"

"No, of course not."

"Handling chocolates is a tricky business. There are very apt to be latent fingerprints on those chocolates."

117

"That's fine. They won't be mine."

"I can depend on that?"

"Definitely. I promise—word of honor."

"How many bags did your husband have when he left?"

"One suitcase."

"What kind?"

"Just an ordinary big suitcase."

"Now wait a minute," Mason said. "He bought a bag somewhere before he got to Fresno."

"I don't know why he should have done that."

"And he had two suitcases with him."

"I don't know where the other one came from. I mean, why he had it with him. He kept the bulk of his things at Paradise. He only carried the things he needed for short stays when he left up there."

"Did he leave any suitcases up at Paradise when you moved?"

"I don't think so. We carried things down in suitcases and left them down in Los Angeles. The suitcases are down there."

"How many of them?"

"Four or five."

"You don't know anything about the two suitcases your husband was carrying?"

"No."

"You don't know what became of them?"

"No."

"Did you know that he was carrying samples of ore in suitcases?"

"No. I suppose he could have."

"Did you know anyone he intended to see on this trip?"

"No. He told me he had a deal on for selling a mine. He was going to make a nice profit if it went through."

"He didn't tell you any more about it?"

"No."

"He didn't talk with you over the telephone from Paradise and give you any more information?"

"No."

"You mean he didn't call you at all from Paradise?"

"Once. That was Sunday. He said he was leaving, that he'd join me Monday night—yesterday."

"That was the only time he called you?"

"Yes."

"Over what period of time?"

"A week or ten days."

"Why didn't he call you more than that?"

"I don't know. I think it was because of Aunt Sara."

"What about her?"

"He thought that she used to listen in on the extension phone. He used to call oftener. Then he said someone was listening and after that he didn't call much. When he did he was very short and curt. He didn't like Aunt Sara."

"And she didn't like him?"

"No."

"Do you know anything about your husband's business affairs?"

"Very little."

"He was going to meet someone and consummate a mining deal?"

"That's what he said."

"Where?"

"I gathered it was up here someplace—either Fresno or Modesto or someplace like that."

"You don't know anyone he intended to meet in San Bernardino?"

"No. He wasn't going to San Bernardino."

"How do you know?"

"He was coming straight home."

"How do you know?"

"He said he was."

"When?"

"When he telephoned."

"The first time he telephoned?"

"There was only once."

"You mean this last trip?"

"Yes."

"Can you describe the suitcase that you packed for him? What it looked like?"

"It was a dark brown leather. It had been scuffed up. It had his initials in gold on it."

Mason pushed back his chair.

"Where are you going?"

"Out and skirmish around," Mason said. "I can find out more outside than I can in here talking to you. You aren't telling me anything."

"That's because I don't know anything."

"Let's hope you can make a jury believe that," Mason told her.

Chapter 10

Mason caught a late train to Los Angeles and entered his office at 10:50 A.M. to find Della Street regarding a letter with puzzled scrutiny.

"Now what?" Mason asked.

"Gosh, Chief, I didn't hear you come in. How was the trip?"

"Okay. The D.A. in Fresno seems to be a nice chap, but he's going to give us quite a fight. What's causing the expression on your face, Della?"

"Was there one?"

"There certainly was," Mason said, walking over to take the letter from her hand. "What is it?"

"It's from the detective in Bakersfield. I had just glanced through it."

"What does he want?"

"Money."

Mason took the letter and read:

Dear Mr. Mason:

I am writing this on my portable typewriter at San Bernardino. I have just learned by radio report that Edward Davenport of Paradise is dead, that his wife is accused of his murder and that you are representing her. I assume that you are also handling the affairs of the estate. I was doing work for Ed Davenport pursuant to his instructions when I learned of his death.

I am not in a position to wait for an estate to be probated before getting my money, and because Mr. Davenport indicated the job I was working on was of considerable importance to him it may be something you as attorney for the estate and for Mrs. Davenport should know about.

Since he is dead I can't gain anything by being loyal to him and if the enclosed report is of value to you and his wife you might remember that I'm open to any employment in my profession in any way I can be of assistance.

I take it my prompt co-operation should entitle me to a prompt remittance from you and I hope the enclosed report will be of value to you.

I am enclosing herewith a bill for $225 covering salary and expense in connection with my employment by Mr. Davenport to cover unit thirteen of the Pacific Palisades Motor Court at San Bernardino.

For your information I had met Mr. Davenport in connection with another business matter which I transacted for him some two years ago in connection with a mining deal. I have not seen him since but presume he had filed my name to be used in connection with any similar matter of employment which he might have.

I shall be most happy to be of any further assistance.

> Very truly yours,
> Beckemeyer Detective Service.
> By Jason L. Beckemeyer.

"Well," Mason said, "we seem to clear up one phase of the mystery only to run onto another mystery. Why the devil did Davenport want to have a detective cover unit thirteen in that motel at San Bernardino?"

"Why did we?" Della Street asked.

"We did because of that telephone call, which, incidentally, must have been received some time after Davenport's death. Let's have a look at the detective's report."

She handed him the typewritten sheet.

Pursuant to instructions received over the telephone at approximately nine-fifteen on the evening of the eleventh from Edward Davenport who telephoned from Fresno, California, identified himself and arranged for the employment, I drove to San Bernardino on the evening of the twelfth to cover unit thirteen of the Pacific Palisades Motor Court.

I arrived at San Bernardino at approximately 1:00 A.M. on the morning of the thirteenth. The Pacific Palisades Motor Court had a sign announcing that there were no vacancies. I parked my automobile in such a position that I could watch the entrance to unit thirteen and kept watch until approximately ten-thirty in the morning, during which time I was on the job personally making absolutely certain that anyone who entered or left unit thirteen would be under surveillance.

At approximately ten-thirty on the morning of the thirteenth I noticed a maid enter the unit with a passkey, after first knocking. The maid had a portable unit containing bed linens, towels, etc., and had been previously engaged in making up units which had been vacated.

I immediately left my automobile, approached unit thirteen, and knocked on the door which had been left ajar. The maid answered the knock and I pushed my way into the unit and stated that I wanted to talk with the maid who had just made up unit ten. Inasmuch as I had seen the same maid emerge from unit ten I knew she was the one I wanted.

She seemed somewhat alarmed and wanted to know my business. I pretended that I was an officer without actually telling her I was, and asked her to describe the condition in which she had found unit ten, how many people had occupied it, whether there was anything that indicated that these people had been using drugs or were engaged in the drug traffic. The maid fell for this story and talked with me at some length. I was able during the conversation to size up unit thirteen. It had not been occupied during the night. By discreet inquiries I learned that the unit had been engaged by telephone the night before and that remittance had been transmitted by telegraph. The maid did not know the name of the person engaging the unit.

Cautioning the maid that under no circumstances was she to mention my visit to anyone—either her employer, her fellow employees or any occupant of the premises—I returned to my automobile and kept unit thirteen under surveillance until six o'clock that evening. I had not been instructed as to what I should do in case the unit was unoccupied, as Mr. Davenport seemed certain it would be occupied on the evening of the twelfth. My instructions were to see who called on the party early on the morning of the thirteenth, and to be on the safe side I decided to go on duty at 1:00 A.M. During this time I convinced myself that no one had checked into the unit. I had provided myself with sandwiches and thermos containers of coffee so that I did not interrupt my surveillance for eating. A conveniently located service station enabled me to keep an almost continuous watch on the unit, and during brief periods when it was out of my observation I assured myself each time that no one had entered the premises.

At about six o'clock on the evening of the thirteenth, while listening to a radio newscast, I learned that Ed Davenport had died the day before, that his widow was being held on suspicion of murder, and that Mr. Perry Mason was her lawyer.

Under the circumstances and since the unit was unoccupied, I determined to try another angle. I went to the telegraph office and insisted that a telegram which I had sent to the Pacific Palisades Motor Court, sending money to reserve a unit, had not been delivered. The person in charge looked up the records, asked me if I was Mr. Stanton and I assured her that I was. The employee then brought a duplicate copy, showing me that a telegraphic remittance sent by Frank L. Stanton of Fresno had been duly delivered. I apologized and left.

If I can be of further service I will hold myself in readiness. I am quite certain that the unit thirteen was unoccupied during the night of the twelfth and thirteenth. Information elicited from the maid was to the effect that if anyone had occupied the cabin during the first part of the evening of the twelfth, or, in fact, at any time after four o'clock in the afternoon, the necessary service work with towels, bedding, etc., would have waited until the maids came on duty at eight-thirty the next morning.

Beckemeyer Detective Service.
By Jason L. Beckemeyer.

"Well," Della Street said, "that checks in with Paul Drake's information."

Mason nodded, said, "Now why the devil would Ed Davenport have been so anxious to find out who occupied that unit, and why did he wire funds to reserve the cabin and then hire a detective to see who occupied the place?"

"It must have been someone that he wanted to trap in some way," Della Street said. "Or someone whose loyalty he suspected."

"But who?"

"Looks like another job for Paul Drake."

"It sure does."

"Mr. Beckemeyer seems anxious to co-operate," she said.

"Most anxious," Mason agreed.

"And in a hurry for his money."

"He sounds hungry. Tell you what you do, Della, send him a check. That will put him under obligations to our side."

"Do I say anything about his offer to be of service?"

"Tell him we may call on him—later."

"Do you want to sign the letter?"

"No, you do it. Pretend you're sending the remittance on your own responsibility. You sign the check on the special account."

She nodded.

"What else is in the mail? Anything?"

"Nothing too important."

"Ring Paul Drake," Mason said. "Ask him to come down right away if he can."

Mason busied himself at reading the mail until Drake's code knock sounded on the door.

Della Street admitted the detective.

Mason said, "Take a look at this, Paul," and handed him the report of the Beckemeyer Detective Service.

Paul Drake gave the matter frowning and careful consideration.

"Well?" Mason asked.

Drake said, "You can search me, Perry."

Mason said, "It becomes very important to find out whether Ed Davenport was actually the one who wired the money to the Pacific Palisades Motor Court. Suppose you can find out, Paul?"

"Under the circumstances it may be a little difficult. There may be a little red tape. In view of the fact that Fresno has decided it has a murder case against Myrna Davenport the authorities won't take kindly to anyone who is digging up information having to do with Davenport. Are you absolutely certain that Frank L. Stanton and Ed Davenport are one and the same?"

"I'm not absolutely certain," Mason said, "but I'm morally certain. The description checks and the license number of the automobile checks, but we'd better get the registration and have an expert on handwriting make a report."

"You stopped in at that motel in Fresno?"

"That's right. Stanton checked in early in the evening. He had two heavy suitcases with him. Presumably they contained ore from a mine and he was working on some sort of a mining deal. He was very anxious to see that the suitcases remained in his possession. He took them into the motel with him. He had also purchased a brand new traveling bag and he unwrapped that in the motel."

"What about the suitcases?"

Mason said, "If they were in his car or in the motel at Crampton the authorities haven't said anything about them."

"Think someone got away with them?"

"I don't know. There's some evidence Davenport was rolled while he was staying in Fresno. If that happened whoever did the job must have taken the suitcases. They may have had valuable ore samples."

"How valuable?"

"That's the point. Even rich ore would hardly be worth all that trouble."

"Unless it was a job of salting a claim somewhere."

"Could be," Mason said. "The district attorney at Fresno, for your information, Paul, is a deadly, two-fisted fighter who isn't going to be easy.

"I think he's a square-shooter. I don't think he'd want to prosecute Myrna Davenport if he didn't think she was guilty. Her preliminary hearing is set for tomorrow."

"Think he'll show his hand?" Drake asked.

"He'll show only enough of it to get her bound over," Mason said. "He's working hand in glove with the district attorney here and the idea is they'll get Mrs. Davenport convicted of the murder of her husband up there. They may or may not get the death penalty. As soon as that case is finished they'll take her down here and make a try for the death penalty in the case of Hortense Paxton. That's going to be a cinch, particularly if they're able to get a conviction of anything from manslaughter on up in the Fresno court."

"You mean they'll drag in both cases?"

"They may have some difficulty connecting up the two cases," Mason said, "even under the liberal rules that are allowed these days for showing a general scheme. The D.A. in Fresno might drag in the Hortense Paxton poisoning under the theory that he was showing motivation for the death of Davenport. The Los Angeles authorities would have a hell of a time dragging the Davenport murder in as part of the Paxton case.

"That's probably why they decided to try her first in Fresno on the murder of her husband. But let her get a conviction in either case and the minute she takes the stand in the other they can impeach her by showing she's been convicted of a felony and letting the jury know what that felony was."

"I get you," Drake said.

"Therefore," Mason said, "it becomes vitally important for us to get the facts and all the facts, and if possible to get them first."

"That's quite an order," Drake told him. "The authorities up there have the inside track. They have all kinds of manpower. They have the authority. They know the ropes."

"I know," Mason said, "but they may not know the importance of getting all the information on Stanton and getting it correlated fast.

"Now here are certain things that are very definitely established. Ed Davenport had something on which he was working, something which was important. His wife probably didn't know anything about it.

"Here's the low-down on that San Bernardino job. While Della and I were up in Paradise the twelfth the telephone rang. It was a pay station from Bakersfield. Della Street answered the phone. A man came on the line and immediately said, 'Pacific Palisades Motor Court at San Bernardino, unit thirteen' and hung up."

"That was absolutely all of the conversation?" Drake asked.

"Every word of it," Mason said.

"Well," Drake said. "It all ties in with the idea that that motel was to have been used for something rather important. Now why would Davenport have paid the rent on it and then kept it under surveillance? Particularly if he intended to occupy it himself."

"His wife is quite certain that he didn't intend to occupy it himself, that he was leaving Fresno and intended to drive straight home."

"You can't depend on what his wife tells you," Drake said. "She's an interested party—and she may be a guilty party."

"There was one thing significant about the call to Paradise," Mason said. "It didn't occur to me at the time. I knew there was something strange about it but the significance didn't dawn on me until later."

"What's that?"

"The man talking from Bakersfield didn't ask if he was talking with Mabel Norge. As soon as Della Street said hello he gave the message.

"Now if it had been Ed Davenport who was calling he would have known that Della Street wasn't Mabel Norge. He would either have detected a difference in the voices or he would have talked enough to have made certain. And, of course, we know now that Ed Davenport was dead when that call was made.

"Moreover," Mason went on, "if it had been anyone delivering a message in accordance with instructions you would have thought that he would have taken some steps to have ascertained the identity of the party to whom he was talking.''

''But he didn't?''

''That's right, he didn't.''

''Why?''

''There's only one solution,'' Mason said. ''He didn't know anything about the setup at Paradise. He didn't know who Mabel Norge was. Her voice meant nothing to him, and her identity meant nothing to him. He simply called up, left a message, and hung up fast.''

Drake thought the matter over, then slowly nodded.

''And there's one more thing,'' Mason said, ''we're going to look up Sara Ansel all the way along the line.''

''Now you're talking,'' Drake agreed.

''Remember,'' Mason told him, ''that as it turned out Sara Ansel received some substantial benefit from the death of Hortense Paxton.''

''Rather indirect,'' Drake said. ''She couldn't have been certain at all that Delano was going to change his will and cut her in.''

''She couldn't have been certain according to any information we have at the present time,'' Mason said, ''but when we get more information we may find she had reason to know what would happen.''

''If she knows you're investigating her she's going to be a handful,'' Drake warned.

''She'll be a handful anyway,'' Mason told him. ''Get what information you can, Paul. Start men working in Fresno and keep them working. We're going to trial tomorrow morning on the preliminary examination.''

''Aren't you letting them rush things a bit?''

''I'm doing the rushing,'' Mason said. ''I want to ask some questions before the D.A. knows the answers.''

''Let's hope the answers don't crucify your client,'' Drake said.

''That,'' Mason told him, ''is why I want you to get busy and keep busy. I don't want to ask the questions that are going to elicit that type of answer.''

Chapter 11

It was quite apparent that whatever mistakes Talbert Vandling, the district attorney of Fresno County, might be about to make, the mistake of underestimating Perry Mason as an adversary was not one of them.

Vandling, cool, courteous, wary and watchful, started putting on his case with that careful thoroughness which characterized a trial before a jury rather than a preliminary hearing before a magistrate.

"My first witness," he said, "will be George Medford."

George Medford turned out to be a nine-year-old boy, freckle-faced, rather embarrassed, with prominent eyes and ears, but who gave the impression of telling the truth.

"Where do you live?" Vandling asked.

"In Crampton."

"How long have you lived there?"

"Three years."

"You are living with your father and mother?"

"Yes, sir."

"What's your father's name?"

"Martin Medford."

"What does he do?"

"He runs a service station."

"In Crampton?"

"Yes, sir."

"Now, George, I'm going to ask you if you went out with your father on the thirteenth to a place about three miles out of Crampton?"

"Yes, sir."

"Were you familiar with that place?"

"Yes, sir."

"Where is it?"

"It's on a little hill up in some kind of brush, sort of. You know, little live oak trees and some shorter brush. I don't know, sagebrush or greasewood I guess, or something. You know, just kind of brush."

"You had been out there before?"

"Yes, sir."

"How did you get out there?"

"I rode my bike."

"Did anyone go out there with you?"

"Yes, sir."

"Who?"

"Jimmy Eaton."

"Jimmy Eaton is a boy about your age?"

"Six months older."

"And how did he get out there?"

"He'd ride his bike."

"Now, why did you go out there, George? What were you doing out there?"

"Oh, just playing."

"Why did you go out there to play?"

"Well, it was a good place to ride our bikes. There's a road near there and cars hardly ever go on it. The folks didn't want us to ride our bicycles on any of the main highways because of the traffic and—well, we used to go out there. There'd been an old house up on the hill and the people had moved away or something and the house had started to cave in and—oh, we just used to go out there and hunt bird eggs and play and talk and things."

"How long had you been going out there?"

"Oh, off and on for about six or eight months."

"Now did you notice that a hole had been dug up there?"

"Yes, sir."

"When did you notice that?"

"Well, the first time we seen it was on Friday."

"That would be Friday, the ninth?" Vandling asked.

"Yes, sir. I guess so. The ninth. Yes."

"And what time did you go out there?"

"Along in the afternoon, about three or four o'clock."

"And what did you see?"

"We saw this hole."

"Can you describe the hole?"

"Well, it was a big hole."

"About how big, George? Now this is important. Can you hold your hands to show about how big?"

The boy held his hands apart.

"Indicating a distance of about three and a half feet," Vandling said. "Now about how long was it?"

"Long enough so you could lie down in it and still have lots of room."

"You mean lie down straight out, stretched out?"

"Yes, sir."

"How deep was it?"

George stood up and placed his hand about even with his stomach. "It came up to here."

"Had you been out there on Thursday, the eighth?"

"No, sir."

"Had you been out there on Wednesday, the seventh?"

"Yes, sir."

"Was that hole there then?"

"No, it wasn't."

"What was there at the place where the hole was?"

"Just ground."

"Now when you went out Friday, at four o'clock, the hole was there?"

"Yes, sir."

"That hole was completed?"

"Yes, sir."

"What kind of a hole was it?"

"A good hole."

"What do you mean by that?"

"Well, it had been made with a shovel so it was straight down. The sides were straight. The corners were good and clear. It was a nice hole."

"What had been done with the dirt which was taken from that hole, George?"

"That dirt had been piled up over on the side."

"Which side?"

"Both sides."

"You mean not on the ends of the hole but on the sides of the hole?"

"Yes, sir."

"And what about the bottom of the hole?"

"It was just nice and even. It was a good hole."

"And this hole was there on Friday, the ninth, in the afternoon?"

"Yes, sir."

"And it was not there on Wednesday?"

"No, sir."

"Were you boys out there Saturday?"

"Yes, sir."

"And what did you do?"

"We played in the hole."

"How did you play in it?"

"Oh, we'd jump down in it, and then we played it was a fort and then we'd lie down so as to be out of sight and see if birds would come close and—oh, we just played."

"Were you out there Sunday?"

"No, sir."

"Did you go out there Monday?"

"No, sir."

"Did you go out there Tuesday, the thirteenth?"

"You mean this last Tuesday?"

"Yes."

"Yes, we went out there."

"And what had happened?"

"Well, the hole had all been filled in."

"So what did you do, if anything?"

"Well, I told my dad that—"

"Never mind what you told anyone, George. What did you do?"

"Well, we played."

"And then what?"

"Then we went home."

"And did you return again that day?"

"Yes, sir."

"How soon after you got home?"

"About an hour afterward."

"Who went with you?"

"My dad and Jimmy."

"And your dad is Martin Medford, the man who is here in court?"

"Yes, sir."

"That's all," Vandling said.

"No questions," Mason said, "at least at the present time. I may state, Your Honor, that with some of these witnesses, where the importance of the testimony is not readily apparent, I might like to recall them for cross-examination if it appears that the testimony should subsequently be connected with matters of importance to the defendant's case."

"These witnesses are all important," Vandling said. "I can assure the Court and counsel of that. I may also assure counsel that the prosecution in this case is just as anxious as the defense to get at the truth of the matter and we will have no objection to counsel recalling any witness that he may desire for any cross-examination at any time, subject only to the fact that the cross-examination must be pertinent."

Judge Siler, the magistrate conducting the hearing, said, "All right, we'll consider that in the nature of a stipulation. Defense has that right."

"My next witness will be Martin Medford," Vandling said.

Martin Medford testified that he was the father of George; that on the late afternoon of the thirteenth the boy had returned and told him about the hole having been filled in; that he had decided that the matter should be looked into, had taken a shovel and driven out to the place, accompanied by his son and Jimmy Eaton; that he had found the soil rather loose over the area indicated and had dug down in the hole; that at a distance of approximately two and a half feet he had encountered a rather yielding obstruction; that he had scraped away the dirt and found that this was the leg of a man; that he had immediately discontinued his digging and rushed to a telephone where he had notified the sheriff.

"Cross-examine," Vandling said.

"You returned to the place with the sheriff?" Mason asked.

"Yes, sir."

"And stood there while the hole was excavated?"

"Yes, sir."

"Did you help in the digging?"

"Yes, sir."

"What was uncovered?"

"The body of a man."

"How was it dressed?"

"In pajamas."

"And that was all?"

"That was all."

"No further questions," Mason said.

The sheriff took the stand, told of going out with two deputies to the location indicated by Martin Medford. There they excavated the dirt which had apparently recently been placed in the hole, that is, the dirt had not settled. It was soft, although there had been some tramping around on the top of the hole.

The body of Edward Davenport had been found buried in the hole. The body had been removed to the morgue. At a later date the sheriff had returned and very carefully excavated the loose dirt in order to find something of the dimensions of the original hole; that the hole was in soil firm enough to retain the imprints of the original digging, and it had been quite apparent that a hole approximately three feet five inches by six feet had been very carefully excavated in the form of a very neat rectangle.

In response to a specific question by Vandling he stated that an attempt had been made to find tracks but that because of the tracks of the boys and of Martin Medford at the time of his digging there had been no footprints which had been deemed significant.

"You may cross-examine," Vandling said.

"Under the circumstances," Mason said, "I will ask no questions at this time."

"Of course," Vandling pointed out, "my stipulation with counsel was for the purpose of enabling him to protect the rights of his client and not to be caught by surprise. It was not a blanket invitation to pass up all cross-examination until all of our case had been presented and then recall witnesses."

"I understand," Mason said. "I can assure counsel I will not take advantage of his courtesy in the matter. I will recall witnesses only when it seems there is some specific point to be gained by so doing."

"Thank you," Vandling said. "That's all, Sheriff."

Dr. Milton Hoxie was the next witness. He gave his qualifications as a physician and surgeon and toxicologist. He testified that he had been called on to perform an autopsy at the morgue on the evening of the thirteenth, that circumstances had prevented him actually performing the autopsy until nearly midnight, when he had been able to leave his practice long enough to perform the autopsy.

He had found the body of a man five feet eight inches tall, weight one hundred forty pounds, who was about thirty-five years of age, who had arteriosclerosis but who had apparently died of poisoning. He had performed certain tests and had detected the presence of a specific poison. He had come to the conclusion that death had been caused by the ingestion of cyanide of potassium. In his opinion at the time of the autopsy the man had been dead for perhaps twenty-four to thirty-six hours.

"Cross-examine," Vandling said abruptly.

"You made a specific test for cyanide of potassium?" Mason asked.

"Yes, sir. Hydrocyanic poisoning."

"And other poisons?"

"I tested for arsenic."

"Did you find any arsenic?"

"Not in significant quantities. No, sir."

"Did you find any quantity at all?"

"Not enough to be of any medical significance."

"Did you find any other poisons?"

"I did not. No, sir."

"Were the vital organs removed from the body?"

"They were. Yes, sir."

"And what was done with them?"

"They were sent to a laboratory at the University of California for additional examination."

"And has a report been received from the University?"

"Not to my knowledge."

"Then you don't know that the man met his death because of the poison you have mentioned?"

"I know that I found enough poison present to result in death and therefore I assume that death was caused by that poison."

"Why did you send the organs to the University of California?"

"Because I wanted to have a more complete check made."

"Because you were looking for some other poison?"

"I thought it would be a good plan to check and see if there was any other poison."

"Then you weren't satisfied that death was caused by potassium cyanide?"

"Certainly I was. But I wanted to see if there were any contributing factors—perhaps there were indications of knockout drops, so-called, or some barbiturate by which the resistance of the man might have been lessened so that the poison could have been administered."

Mason thought that over frowningly.

"Proceed," Judge Siler said.

"Just a moment, Your Honor," Mason said. "I think this opens up an entirely new field here."

"I don't see how," Judge Siler said.

Mason said, "It is apparent that originally the sheriff's office had some theory as to the manner in which the poison was administered and that something in the findings of Dr. Hoxie was not in accordance with that theory."

"Well, I certainly fail to see it," Judge Siler said. "Proceed with your examination."

"Certainly," Mason smiled. "Did you look for evidences of chocolate in the man's stomach, Doctor?"

"I did. I tried to check the stomach contents carefully."

"And what did you find?"

"I found that the man had died approximately an hour after ingesting a meal of bacon and eggs. I did not find any appreciable amount of chocolate."

"Did you test the body for blood alcohol, Doctor?"

"I did."

"What did you find?"

"I found 0.15 per cent of alcohol."

"Can you interpret that in terms of its medical significance?"

Dr. Hoxie said, "According to the authorities, at 0.1 per cent a person is normal according to ordinary observation. He has, however, begun to show certain evidences of medical intoxication. At 0.2 per cent he has become intoxicated. He has emotional instability. His inhibitions are greatly diminished. At 0.3 per cent there is a very definite confusion, a staggering gait, a blurred speech. At 0.4 per cent there is stupor, a marked decrease in response to external stimuli and approaching paralysis. From 0.5 per cent to 0.6 per cent there is complete coma and impairment of circulation. There is danger of death which is virtually inevitable after 0.6 per cent of alcohol is in the blood. C. W. Muehlberger has prepared an interesting chart. 0.1 per cent is called 'Dry and Decent.' 0.2 per cent 'Delighted and Devilish.' 0.3 per cent 'Dizzy and Delirious.' 0.4 per cent 'Dazed and Dejected.' 0.5 per cent 'Dead Drunk.' ''

"So in this body in which you found 0.15 per cent of alcohol, what are your conclusions with reference to intoxication?"

"The man had begun to be intoxicated. He was entering the stage described by Muehlberger as 'Delighted and Devilish.' ''

"He would be feeling the effects of alcohol?"

"He would."

"He would be showing some manifestation of those effects?"

"In all probability to the casual observer. Certainly to the trained observer."

"I take it, Doctor," Mason said casually, "that while you were primarily interested at the time of the post-mortem examination in determining the cause of death, you took some steps to identify the body?"

"That is right. I may state that I was present when some steps were taken."

"There is no question in your mind but what the body was that of Edward Davenport?"

"No question at all."

"Let me ask you a hypothetical question, Doctor. Assuming that this man had been poisoned by cyanide of potassium taken in the form of a candy such as was found in the box of candy located among Mr. Davenport's effects at the motel in Crampton, wouldn't death have been almost immediate?"

"It would have been very rapid."

"There was, in other words, enough cyanide in each piece of candy to have resulted in almost immediate death?"

"Not in each piece of candy, Mr. Mason. Some of them contained arsenic and—"

"I'm not trying to trap you, Doctor. I am referring to the candies which contained cyanide."

"That is correct. Yes, sir."

"The development of symptoms and unconsciousness comes very rapidly after the ingestion of doses of cyanide such as you found in the candies which did contain cyanide?"

"Yes, sir."

"Now then, Doctor, if the decedent had met his death from eating a piece of that poisoned candy, wouldn't you have found some chocolate in his stomach?"

"Well, there, of course," Dr. Hoxie said, "is a puzzling situation. I would assume so."

"And did you find such evidences of chocolate?"

"No."

"You would have expected to find some if the man had eaten a piece of poisoned candy?"

"Frankly, I would—unless he might have bitten into the candy which could have caused his death, detected a strange flavor, and have spit out the candy, yet swallowed enough of the poisoned liquid in the candy to have caused death. I assume that is what happened. I think from all the facts it is what must have happened, but I can't find any physical evidence which will enable me to testify it did happen. And I don't see how he could possibly have ingested the poison I found in his stomach unless he had eaten an entire piece of candy at the very least.''

''Then you don't actually know how the man ingested the poison which caused his death?''

''No, sir.''

''How long had he been dead?''

''I am unable to determine. I would say somewhere around twenty-four to thirty-six hours.''

''What about a condition known as rigor mortis, Doctor?''

''At the time I made the examination rigor mortis was well marked in the thighs and legs but the neck and shoulders were limp.''

''What about post-mortem lividity?''

''That was well developed, indicating that the position of the body had been unchanged after death, that is, within a short time after death.''

''Now as I understand it, rigor mortis develops first in the face and jaws, then gradually extends downward?''

''That is correct.''

''And it leaves the body in the same way?''

''Yes, sir.''

''How long does it take rigor mortis to develop?''

''It varies. But under ordinary circumstances from eight to twelve hours.''

''Now in this case rigor mortis had not only developed but had enveloped the entire body, then it had begun to disappear. Is that correct?''

''That is substantially true, yes.''

''According to the authorities I believe that the envelopment of the entire body in rigor mortis is supposed to take about eighteen hours?''

''It varies.''

Mason said, ''Are you familiar with the writings of Dr. LeMoyne Snyder?''

''Yes, sir.''

''I believe that in his book, *Homicide Investigation*, Dr. LeMoyne Snyder considers a hypothetical case such as you have described where rigor mortis is still well marked in the thighs and legs, and estimates such a situation as indicating that death took place from twenty-nine to thirty-four hours previously.''

"I am not entirely familiar with his schedule on that.''

"But you would say that that was substantially correct?''

"I would say it could well be, yes.''

"Now you are referring to the condition of the body at the time you performed the post-mortem?''

"That is correct.''

"And you did not perform the post-mortem until some hours after the body had been discovered?''

"That is true.''

"I believe you said your post-mortem was performed about midnight?''

"Yes, sir.''

"And you're referring to the condition of the body at the time you saw it?''

"Yes, sir.''

"So, generally speaking, the man must have met his death at from two o'clock in the afternoon to seven o'clock in the evening of the preceding day, which was Monday, the twelfth. Is that correct?''

"Well, that is correct if you are going to take such a time chart, but rigor mortis is exceedingly variable. It depends upon temperature. It depends upon certain conditions. I have seen rigor mortis develop almost immediately when death has occurred after a struggle under conditions of temperature which—''

"Were there any evidences of struggle in this case?''

"No, there were not.''

"You wouldn't care to fix a definite time by the development of rigor mortis?''

"Not definitely.''

"But you do know that such an authority as Dr. LeMoyne Snyder has claimed that under ordinary circumstances the development of rigor mortis such as you observed in the body at this time would have indicated that death had occurred between the hours of two o'clock and seven o'clock of the preceding day?''

"Yes, sir. I guess so.''

"Not what you guess, Doctor, but what you know."

"Yes, that is true."

"Had you considered this fact as being a development in the case?"

"Frankly, I had not."

"Why, Doctor?"

"Because of the fact that a doctor certified the time of death as being between two and three o'clock in the afternoon of the day preceding, and there is nothing in the schedule of rigor mortis which can be narrowed down definitely. Dr. Snyder and other authorities are dealing only with average cases. They can't lay down rules which can definitely determine the time of death in any individual case. They are talking in terms of generalities, and there is nothing more tricky, or I may say nothing which offers more of a variable under existing conditions, than the development of rigor mortis."

"You are familiar with the symptoms of arsenic poisoning, Doctor?"

"Yes, sir."

"And what are those symptoms?"

"Generally there is a burning of the mouth and the throat. There are abdominal cramps with nausea and vomiting. There is usually diarrhea. There are times under certain circumstances when the first symptoms are somewhat delayed, but as a rule the first symptoms are very rapid in their development after the ingestion of the poison."

"Thank you, Doctor," Mason said. "I have no further questions."

Vandling said, "Call Harold Titus to the stand."

Titus came forward, was sworn, testified that he was a deputy sheriff, that he had specialized in the study of fingerprints, that he had been present at the time when the body of Edward Davenport was discovered in the grave about three miles out of Crampton, that he had taken fingerprints of the dead man, and that he had compared a thumbprint with that on the driving license issued to Edward Davenport and that the prints were identical.

"Had you previously made an investigation in a motor court at Crampton in connection with this case?"

"I had. Yes, sir."

"What time was that investigation made?"

"About half-past three on the afternoon of the twelfth."

"That was Monday?"

"Yes, sir."

"What did you discover?"

"I discovered a locked room in which a corpse was supposed to be located. The door was opened and there was no corpse in the room. There was no one in the room. There was an open window and a loosened screen. There were men's clothes in the room. There was a handbag, a box of candy. There was a wallet containing various papers of identification indicating that the room had been occupied by one Edward Davenport."

"Did you meet the defendant, Myrna Davenport, at that time?"

"I did. Yes, sir."

"And did she make any statements to you with reference to the identity of the man who had occupied that unit?"

"Yes, sir."

"Who did she say the man was?"

"Edward Davenport, her husband."

"What did she say about his condition?"

"That he was in a dying condition when she and her companion, a Mrs. Ansel, arrived."

"Did she say whether she and Mrs. Ansel had been admitted to the room?"

"Yes. She said that they both went into the room, that afterward she had retired, that shortly afterward her husband had taken a turn for the worse, that his respiration was very shallow, that he was barely breathing, that the doctor was called and announced that the man's condition was very serious. The doctor had been with him when he died. The doctor had then locked up the room after having stated that the circumstances of the death were such that he could not sign a death certificate."

"Did she make any further statements?"

"There were some statements to the effect that the conduct of the doctor had indicated to her mind that he was insinuating she had murdered her husband and she naturally resented that."

"And what was your position in the matter at that time?"

Titus grinned and said, "We learned that Edward Davenport was a heavy drinker. We skirmished around and found a witness who'd seen someone in the same patterned pajamas the man was wearing climb out of the window of that unit, and so we decided the fellow had got hold of some alcohol and had gone off on a binge."

"Then what did you do?"

"Well, at the insistence of Dr. Renault, we retained the key to the room in question while we made an additional investigation."

"Was any restraint placed upon the movements of the defendant or her companion, Mrs. Ansel?"

"Definitely not."

"And what did they do?"

"They were located in another unit of the motel."

"You didn't give them a key to the cabin?"

"Definitely not."

"You retained that key?"

"Yes, sir."

"Now was any attempt made to place the defendant under surveillance?"

"Not at that time. Later on there was."

"What happened?"

"Well, she told us she was going to stay on overnight at the motel, but about—oh, I don't know, around seven o'clock the manager of the motel phoned us that she and Mrs. Ansel had left. We traced them to Fresno and found they had taken a plane to San Francisco."

"What did you do?"

"We telephoned San Francisco to pick her up when the plane landed and put a tail on her."

"And that was done?"

"Well, of course, I only know now from reports."

"I understand. I will not ask you what was done by anyone else. Now when did you next see the defendant?"

"That was on the fourteenth."

"At what time?"

"At four-thirty in the afternoon."

"And where did you see her?"

"In your office."

"You had a conversation with her?"

"I did."

"And generally what did the defendant state to you at that time with reference to a box of candy which had been produced?"

"She stated that she had purchased that box of candy and had placed it in her husband's traveling bag, that the husband always carried a box of candy with him, that he was a heavy drinker and a periodic drinker. There were times when he felt the craving for alcohol and when he was able to eat candy, and by going on what she called a candy binge, could control the craving for alcohol."

"She admitted to you that she had bought this box of candy?"

"Yes, sir."

"Did you ask her at that time whether she had in any way opened the box or tampered with the chocolates?"

"She told me that she had simply purchased the box of chocolates and had placed it in her husband's bag, unopened, as it came from the candy store. That she had taken off the outer wrappings because she had purchased two boxes at the same time, but that she had not disturbed the cellophane wrapper around the box."

"Did you examine that box of chocolates?"

"Yes, sir."

"For the purpose of determining latent fingerprints?"

"Yes, sir."

"What did you discover?"

"I found two chocolates which had the prints of the defendant's right thumb and right forefinger."

"Were you able to photograph those prints?"

"Yes, sir."

"Do you have the photographs with you?"

"I have."

"Please show them to defendant's counsel and then I'm going to ask that they be received in evidence."

"No objection," Mason said, hastily inspecting the photographs.

"Later on, were you present when those pieces of candy bearing the latent fingerprints were tested for poison?"

"I was."

"And did you in some way designate those particular pieces of chocolate?"

"Yes, sir. We pasted a small piece of paper on the bottom of those chocolates, numbering one of them number one and the other number two. I placed my initials in ink on that piece of paper."

"And those two chocolates in your presence were tested for poison?"

"Yes, sir."

"Cross-examine," Vandling said.

Mason said conversationally, "Do you know what was found with reference to the presence of poison in those two pieces of chocolate?"

"Only by hearsay."

"That is hearsay from the toxicologist who performed the test?"

"Yes, sir."

"But you were there at the time?"

"Yes, sir."

"What did he say?"

"He said that both of those pieces of chocolate contained cyanide of potassium, that all of the other pieces of chocolate contained arsenic."

"You know that arsenic usually produces death rather slowly?"

"Yes, sir."

"And that cyanide produces it very rapidly?"

"Yes, sir."

"Did you make any attempt as an investigating officer to determine why two pieces of candy containing poison which

146

would bring about almost instantaneous death had been mixed with candy which would bring about a slow death?''

''No, sir. I asked the defendant about that and she insisted all of the time that she had not opened the box of candy, that she had never touched any of the chocolates.''

''That's all,'' Mason said. ''No further questions.''

''I will now call Sara Ansel to the stand,'' Vandling said.

Sara Ansel, who had been in the back of the courtroom, stood up and said belligerently, ''I don't want to be a witness in this case. I don't know anything that would be of the slightest help to the prosecution. That young woman who is being tried is my sister's niece and the poor girl is innocent.''

''Just come forward and be sworn,'' Vandling said.

''I've told you that I don't want to be a witness. I—''

''Come forward and be sworn, madam,'' Judge Siler announced, and, as Sara Ansel still hesitated, said, ''Otherwise you will be tried for contempt of court. This is a court of law. You were called as a witness. You are present. Now come forward.''

Slowly Sara Ansel marched down the aisle, through the swinging gate in the section reserved for attorneys and witnesses, and up to the witness box. She held up her right hand, was sworn, smiled reassuringly at Myrna, then sat down and glared at Vandling.

''You're Sara Ansel?'' Vandling said. ''You are at the present time living in Los Angeles with the defendant in this case in a house which was formerly the property of William C. Delano. Is that right?''

''That's right,'' she snapped.

''How were you related to William C. Delano?''

''I wasn't related, that is, not actually. My sister married William Delano's brother.''

''They are both dead?''

''Both dead.''

''What relatives did Delano have at the time of his death?''

''He had none at the time of his death other than Myrna, unless you could call me a relative by marriage.''

''You were his sister-in-law?''

''In a way, yes.''

"He referred to you as such?"

"Yes."

"You had seen William C. Delano several times in his lifetime?"

"Several times."

"Now shortly before his death did you see him?"

"Yes."

"How long before his death?"

"Approximately a month."

"Now can you describe generally the condition of William Delano's household during that month? Who was there?"

"I was there, and his niece, Hortense Paxton, was there, and Myrna and Ed Davenport. Myrna came to help with the work."

"And what happened to Hortense Paxton?"

"She died."

"And after that William Delano died?"

"Yes."

"About how long after Hortense Paxton's death was it that William Delano died?"

"A little over two weeks."

"During that two weeks he was a very sick man?"

"Yes."

"And he changed his will, that is, he made a new will during that time?"

"I don't know."

"Didn't he tell you in the presence of the defendant, Myrna Davenport, that he was making a new will?"

"Not in so many words. Lawyers came to the house and he was executing a document. He was a very sick man."

"Under the terms of that will you inherited some money, did you not?"

"That's none of your business."

"Under the terms of that last will you inherited some money, did you not?"

"Answer the question," Judge Siler said.

"Yes, sir," she snapped.

"How much?"

"A hundred thousand dollars and a fifth interest in his big house."

"When did you first meet the defendant, Myrna Davenport?"

"When I came to visit William Delano."

"Was she living there at the house at that time?"

"Not at that time. She was there helping with the work, helping Hortense, but—"

"Now just a moment. By saying that she was helping Hortense you mean she was helping Hortense Paxton, the niece who died?"

"Yes."

"And Hortense Paxton was running the house, supervising the servants, waiting on William Delano?"

"Yes."

"And had been for some time?"

"She'd been living with him for more than two years. She was his favorite. They were very close."

"And shortly after you arrived at the house to visit William Delano, the defendant, Myrna Davenport, came to live with him? Isn't that right?"

"Well, it wasn't that simple. That is, you can't divide it into periods like that. Myrna first came to visit and help Hortie—"

"Now, by Hortie you mean Hortense Paxton?"

"Naturally."

"Very well. Go on."

"She was there visiting and helping, and then she decided to move in, that—well, it may have been shortly before I came or shortly afterward, I don't remember which, but in any event, she and Ed, that was her husband, did move in and take up their residence."

"But Mr. Davenport still continued to maintain his office at the place he and Myrna Davenport had been using as a residence up in Paradise in this state?"

"Yes."

"How much of the time?"

"Quite a bit of it."

"After you came, and shortly after Delano's death, Mr. Davenport started absenting himself from home, did he not?"

"What do you mean by home?"

"At that time it was the residence in which William Delano had passed away, was it not?"

"I guess so, yes."

"That's what I mean by his home. I will refer to the place in Paradise as his mining office."

"Very well."

"And shortly after you moved in you noticed that Mr. Davenport began to absent himself, did you not?"

She said, "I don't know what you're trying to get at, but I'll tell you frankly that Ed Davenport and I didn't get along. But that didn't have anything to do with those trips of his. Ed Davenport didn't like me. There wasn't any secret made about that, although I was just as nice to him as I could be, but he thought I was turning Myrna against him. Actually all I was doing was trying to tell Myrna to wake up to what was happening."

"What was happening?"

"He was mingling every cent of Myrna's money he could get hold of with his money and mixing it all up and juggling the assets around so that a body couldn't tell anything in the world about it. If you'd start asking him about his mining properties or what he was doing, or about how much money Myrna had, or what he was doing with it and where it was invested, he'd either clam up on you or jump up and leave the room. Then shortly afterward he'd take another of his 'business trips.' If you *really* tried to pin him down you'd get all sorts of evasive answers. You couldn't tell which was which. I knew what he was doing and he knew I knew what he was doing."

Sara Ansel glowered belligerently at Vandling.

"You knew what he was doing?"

"Certainly I knew what he was doing. I wasn't born yesterday."

"How did you know what he was doing?"

"Why, by asking him questions and getting his answers and seeing the way he was acting and all of that stuff."

"And did he know that you knew what he was doing?"

"Certainly he did. I didn't make any secret of it. That is, I asked him very pointed questions."

"In front of his wife?"

"Naturally. She was the one I was trying to get to wake up."

"And then you talked with his wife privately?"

"Yes."

"And suggested that she should consult an attorney?"

"Yes."

"And what else?"

"That she should hire private detectives to trail him. He was gallivanting around the country. He'd tell Myrna to pack up a suitcase for him, talking to her just as though she were a servant, and tell her he was going off to one of the mines. He wouldn't even tell her which one. He'd say 'one of the mines.'"

"He had several?"

"He did after he began to get his hands on her money. That was when he started to expand. And, as I say, he just mixed transactions around so you couldn't tell anything about anything."

"He was using his wife's money?"

"Of course he was. He didn't have any money of his own. All he had were some mines he was buying and operating on a shoestring. As soon as William Delano died he started in being a big operator right away. He borrowed what money he could on the strength of the money that was coming to his wife. He got his wife to make a big loan at the bank and then he hurried through some kind of partial distribution of the estate so that Myrna could get money, and as soon as it hit Myrna's bank account he drew it right out."

"Do you know how he handled those transactions? Did he give Mrs. Davenport a note or anything?"

"Certainly not. He simply had her put money in a joint account. And all she could ever use that joint account for was just household expenses and an occasional dress or something."

"So you warned Mrs. Davenport about this?"

"Certainly."

"So at a time, say a week ago, Myrna Davenport had every reason to distrust her husband, to hate her husband and to wish him out of the way, did she not?"

"Now what are you getting at? You're putting words in my mouth."

"I'm simply summarizing what you've told me. You had told Mrs. Davenport that her husband was embezzling her money?"

"Yes."

"That he was running around with other women?"

"I suspected it."

"That he was simply trying to get his hands on her inheritance so that he could add it to his own funds and juggle things around so she would lose out financially?"

"Well, I didn't use exactly those words."

"But that was the idea you conveyed?"

"Yes."

"Some ten days ago Edward Davenport announced that he was going to his office in Paradise?"

"Yes."

"And asked his wife to pack his bag?"

"Yes."

"Was anything said about candy?"

"He told her that he needed some fresh candy, that he had eaten up all but one or two pieces in the other box."

"Do you know of your own knowledge what Mrs. Davenport did in connection with packing the bag or getting the candy?"

"Not of my own knowledge. I learned afterward that she bought two boxes of candy."

"And that one box of candy was put in his suitcase?"

"I believe so. I didn't see that with my own eyes."

"Did you know anything about Mrs. Davenport having poisons?"

"She's a great gardener and she did some experimenting with different sprays that she mixed up. She followed some sort of a recipe for plant sprays."

"Did she have arsenic and cyanide of potassium?"

"I don't know."

"Did you talk with her about poison at any time?"

"Well, yes."

"And did she tell you that she had arsenic and cyanide of potassium?"

"She told me that she had some things for sprays."

"Did she tell you she had arsenic and cyanide of potassium?"

Mason said, "Your Honor, this seems to be an attempt on the part of counsel to cross-examine his own witness."

"She's a hostile witness," Vandling said.

"Objection overruled," Judge Siler said. "It's quite apparent that she's a hostile witness."

"Did she tell you she had cyanide of potassium and arsenic?" Vandling asked.

"Yes."

"Did she discuss with you the fact that she had tried to conceal those poisons and bury them so that the authorities couldn't find them?"

There was a long silence.

"Answer the question," Vandling said.

"Yes," Sara Ansel said.

"And you actually saw her burying some of those packages containing poison?"

"She didn't want to be subjected to a lot of inquiry and—"

"Did you actually see her burying those poisons?"

"I saw her digging a hole. I don't know what she put in the hole."

"Did she tell you what she put in the hole?"

"Yes."

"What did she say she put in the hole?"

"Poisons."

"Now then, directing your attention to Monday, the twelfth. You and Mrs. Davenport were at the Delano house?"

"Yes."

"And at some time in the morning, around nine o'clock, you received a telephone call from a doctor in Crampton, did you not—a Dr. Herkimer C. Renault?"

"Yes. The call came through."

"Did you talk on that call or did Myrna Davenport?"

"I did."

"And what did Dr. Renault tell you?"

"He asked for Mrs. Davenport. I told him that I was Myrna Davenport's aunt and that I could take any message to her. He said it was serious news concerning her husband."

"Now as far as the telephone conversation itself was concerned," Vandling said to Judge Siler, "I think that probably is hearsay evidence, but as far as what this witness told the defendant concerning that telephone conversation it goes to the defendant's knowledge and state of mind—"

"I'm not making any objection," Mason interrupted. "Go right ahead."

"Very well. What did that conversation consist of?"

"Dr. Renault told me that Mr. Davenport was in a motel in Crampton, that he was very seriously ill, very, very ill; that he understood the man had high blood pressure and hardening of the arteries, and that he thought it was advisable for Mrs. Davenport to get there just as soon as possible."

"Now I won't waste time with a lot of details," Vandling said, "but you and Mrs. Davenport promptly packed up, made arrangements to catch a plane which would get you into Fresno shortly after noon. You grabbed a taxicab and then you persuaded Mrs. Davenport that she should stop at the office of an attorney, and you did stop at the office of Perry Mason, did you not?"

"Yes, sir."

"Now prior to that time you had some knowledge of the fact that Mr. Davenport had left a letter of some sort, to be delivered to the officers in the event of his death?"

"He had accused Myrna of—well, of lots of things, and he said that he had left a letter to be delivered to the officers in case anything happened to him."

"And you went to the office of Perry Mason with Mrs. Davenport, and Mr. Mason was retained to go to Paradise and get that letter so that it would not be delivered to the officers in the event of Mr. Davenport's death? Isn't that true?"

"Now there, Your Honor," Mason said, "I'm forced to interpose an objection because it calls for a confidential communication between a client and an attorney."

"*You* didn't employ Mr. Mason, did you?" Vandling asked Sara Ansel.

"Me? Certainly not. What would I want with a lawyer?"

"But Myrna Davenport did?"

"She told him what to do."

"And you told him what to do, didn't you?"

"Well, Myrna was pretty well shaken up and—"

"And you told him what to do, didn't you?"

"Well, perhaps I explained certain things to him."

"And you were present at all of the conversation?"

"Yes."

"Tell us what was said at that conversation."

"I object," Mason said. "It's calling for a confidential communication."

"Not with a third person there," Vandling said.

Judge Siler said, "This question calls for the instructions that were given Mr. Mason as an attorney by Mrs. Davenport as a client?"

"Yes, Your Honor, in the presence of Sara Ansel, a third person."

"I don't think it's admissible," Judge Siler said.

"May the Court please, I have authorities on the subject," Vandling said. "I think it is quite clearly admissible."

"Well, I'll study the authorities," Judge Siler said, "but I'll want to take a little time to look them over. I don't like the idea of introducing evidence of what a client told a lawyer."

"I will give Your Honor the authorities and you can—"

"Well now, wait a minute," Judge Siler said. "Why don't I look those up during the noon hour? Why do you have to bring this question up at this time? Can't you withdraw this witness and put on another witness?"

"Yes, I suppose I could," Vandling said.

"Very well. Why not withdraw this witness? We have a question. We have Mr. Mason's objection to the question. You have some authorities on the point. After the noon recess

155

I'll rule on the question and then the witness can either answer or not, depending on my ruling, and the attorney for the defense can proceed with his cross-examination."

"Very well," Vandling said. "Step down, Mrs. Ansel. You may leave the stand."

Sara Ansel heaved herself up out of the witness stand, glared at Vandling.

"But don't leave the city," Vandling warned. "Remember you are under subpoena. You are to remain in attendance here in court during all of the sessions and you are to be here following the noon adjournment."

"Yes," Judge Siler said. "You are under subpoena. Don't try to leave. You are to be here during the entire trial. Do you understand?"

She studied him contemptuously.

"Do you?" Judge Siler asked, raising his voice and showing some irritation.

"Yes," she said.

"See that you're here then," Judge Siler said. "Call your next witness, Mr. Vandling."

"I will now call Dr. Renault to the stand."

Dr. Renault, a slender man about fifty years of age, his manner precisely, coldly professional, took the witness stand and surveyed the district attorney with dark eyes that held no expression whatever. His manner was the carefully cultivated professional manner of a physician who has been on the witness stand before and, while preparing to weigh questions and answers carefully, has a certain professional superiority.

"Your name is Dr. Herkimer Corrison Renault?" Vandling asked.

"That's right. Yes, sir."

"You are licensed to practice in this state as a general practitioner, a doctor of medicine?"

"Yes, sir."

"Oh, we'll stipulate the doctor's qualifications subject to the right to cross-examine," Mason said.

"Where do you practice, Doctor?"

"In Crampton."

"And have been there for how long?"

"About three years."

"On the morning of the twelfth you were called on to administer to a patient who was staying at a motel in Crampton?"

"Yes, sir."

"Who was that patient?"

"Edward Davenport."

"Did you know him at the time?"

"No, sir."

"Did you see the body of Edward Davenport after it was exhumed and prior to autopsy?"

"Yes, sir."

"Were you present at the autopsy?"

"No, sir."

"Was the body that you saw the body of the person you had treated on the twelfth?"

"Yes, sir."

"Did you talk with the defendant on the twelfth of this month?"

"Yes, sir."

"Did she see the person whom you were treating?"

"Yes, sir."

"Did she make any identification of that person?"

"Yes, sir."

"Who did she say it was?"

"She identified him as being Edward Davenport, her husband."

"Now I want you to state exactly what happened in regard to your treatment and in regard to Mr. Davenport's condition."

"Well," Dr. Renault said, "I can't do that very well without telling you what the patient told me."

"I assume, Your Honor," Vandling said, "that there will be some question as to this conversation. I have gathered authorities and am prepared to argue the point. The statements made by the deceased at that time were part of the *res gestae*. At that time they were not what we would call dying declarations within the strict sense of the word, but they were part of the *res gestae* and I submit that the doctor's testimony should be admitted.''

''There isn't any objection,'' Mason said, smiling. ''Go right ahead.''

Vandling smiled. ''I can see, Your Honor, that counsel is playing a shrewd game. He wishes us to tip our hand as fully as possible.''

''I want to get at the facts,'' Mason said.

''And I want to get the facts in,'' Vandling retorted.

''Then there's no occasion for argument,'' the judge rebuked. ''Counsel may refrain from these personalities. Let's get at the facts in the case. Answer the question, Doctor. Tell us what happened and you can tell us what he said.''

Dr. Renault said, ''He told me that he had eaten a chocolate and had become terribly ill, that his wife was trying to poison him.''

''Did he say when he had eaten a chocolate?''

''At about seven o'clock in the morning.''

''What time was it when you saw him?''

''Between eight and nine.''

''Did he associate the chocolate with his sickness?''

''He did.''

''And just what did he tell you about it?''

''He told me that his wife had poisoned one of her relatives in order to get some money from a dying uncle, that he had recently discovered evidence that indicated she had done the poisoning and that she was intending to get rid of him, that he had tried to take precautions and that he had left a letter so that if anything happened to him the authorities would know what had happened.''

''What did you do?''

''At first I treated him for food poisoning. I thought that his ideas might have become exaggerated. Then I began to think that perhaps he actually had been poisoned. In any event, the man kept sinking, and when it appeared to me his condition was serious I telephoned for his wife. She came up and had with her a relative.''

''You told them that Mr. Davenport was dying?''

''I told them he was seriously ill.''

"And what happened?"

"Some time between two and three o'clock they called me and I rushed down to the motel. I entered the room and found Mr. Davenport dying."

"Then what happened?"

"I took his pulse. I tried to give him a heart stimulant but he didn't respond. He became weaker and suddenly died."

"And what did you do, if anything?"

"I told Mrs. Davenport that under the circumstances I couldn't sign a medical certificate, that I would have to take steps to preserve the evidence. I locked the door and left."

"And then what did you do?"

"I notified the authorities."

"And then what?"

"When I returned with the authorities the corpse had been moved."

"Just a moment, Doctor," Vandling said. "You say the corpse had been moved?"

"Exactly," Dr. Renault announced with scientific precision. "The corpse had been moved." He waited a moment and then repeated slowly, with emphasis on each word, *"The corpse had been moved."*

"What makes you say that, Doctor?"

"Because corpses don't get up and walk away."

"You're satisfied that Mr. Davenport was dead?"

"I know he was dead. I saw him die."

"There have been cases where mistakes have been made, where a condition of coma has been mistakenly diagnosed as death?"

"I suppose so. I have never made such a mistake. I think that you will find that all of those mistakes are made when a man has been found in a cataleptic condition, or a condition of suspended animation, and the medical practitioner has been misled into assuming that death had taken place. In other words, I don't think those conditions exist where a medical man is standing by a patient and actually sees death take place."

"How long were you gone?" Vandling asked. "That is, how long was it from the time you announced to Mrs. Davenport that her husband had died and left the place before you returned with the authorities?''

''I presume it was something like an hour.''

''Then you are prepared to say that Mr. Davenport was dead—at what hour, Doctor?''

''I am prepared to say that he died between two-thirty and three o'clock in the afternoon. I didn't notice my watch particularly, but it was about that time. I am prepared to state definitely that some person or persons moved his body from the place where he died and where I had left the body, before I returned about an hour later with the officers.''

''Cross-examine,'' Vandling said.

Mason said, ''Doctor, let's get this straight. You first saw Ed Davenport between eight and nine in the morning?''

''That's correct.''

''He told you that he was taken ill about seven o'clock in the morning?''

''Yes, sir.''

''And what were his symptoms when you first treated him?''

''He was suffering from extreme weakness, a condition bordering on collapse.''

''Were any symptoms of arsenic poisoning present?''

''Not at that time. He told me that he had lost everything he had eaten, that he had been purging and vomiting, that he was feeling cold all over and that there were abdominal cramps.''

''Those were not the symptoms of arsenic poisoning?''

''I will say, Mr. Mason, that if the man had ingested arsenic poisoning at say a little before seven o'clock in the morning, that if the condition of his body had been such that a large dose of poison induced almost instantaneous nausea, it is quite possible that the regurgitation of the poison which had been ingested could have been sufficiently complete so that the symptoms would have been those as I found them.''

''Then at that time Davenport told you that he suspected his wife of trying to poison him?''

''Very definitely.''

''That he had eaten a piece of candy from a box that had

160

been placed in his bag by his wife and that he was satisfied he had been poisoned from that piece of candy?''

"Yes, sir.''

"Did he tell you how it happened that he ate a piece of candy at around seven o'clock in the morning?''

"Yes, sir. He told me that he was sometimes a heavy drinker, that quite frequently when he had this overwhelming urge for alcohol that sometimes he could control it by eating large quantities of sweets.''

"So,'' Mason said, "as soon as he became ill he suspected the candy?''

"Well, he didn't say that in so many words but I gathered that was the general situation. Yes, sir.''

"And he was in a condition of shock, of extreme depression when you saw him?''

"Yes, sir.''

"And he showed no improvement?''

"No, sir.''

"You thought it was possible the end would come?''

"Yes, sir.''

"From this debilitation and shock rather than from arsenic poisoning?''

"Yes, sir, in view of his general physical condition.''

"So you called his wife?''

"Yes, sir.''

"Are you familiar with the symptoms of poisoning from cyanide of potassium?''

"Yes, sir.''

"Now then,'' Mason said, "how does it happen, Doctor, or, rather, how do you account for the fact that if this man suspected at nine o'clock in the morning that the first piece of candy was poisoned that he would have taken another piece of candy at three o'clock in the afternoon?''

"Oh, just a moment,'' Vandling said. "That question is argumentative.''

"I'm trying to test the doctor's opinion,'' Mason said.

Judge Siler, who seemed to adopt a rather passive position, hoping that counsel would get matters straightened out, looked from one to the other.

"He didn't," Dr. Renault snapped.

"Didn't what?" Mason asked.

"Didn't take another piece of candy."

Vandling made a little gesture with his hands, sat down and smiled, said, "Well, go ahead. The doctor seems to be doing very well."

"You have heard the testimony of Dr. Hoxie that the man died of poisoning by cyanide of potassium?"

"Yes, sir."

"Do you have any quarrel with that statement?"

"It is not my province to quarrel with any condition found by the pathologist in making a post-mortem."

"Well," Mason said, "did the man die of cyanide poisoning? You saw him die. You know the symptoms. Did he exhibit symptoms of poisoning by cyanide?"

"No, sir, he did not."

"He did not?" Mason asked.

Dr. Renault set his jaw firmly. "He did not," he said.

"Then you don't think poison caused his death?"

"Now, just a moment, Mr. Mason. That's another matter. I do think poison caused his death."

"But you don't think it was cyanide of potassium?"

"No, sir, I do not. I think his death resulted from extreme shock following the ingestion of arsenic poisoning which had been largely eliminated from the system."

"Now wait a minute," Mason said. "You were the attending physician. You saw the man die."

"Yes, sir."

"And you don't think his death was caused by cyanide of potassium?"

"No, sir. I do not."

"Now just a moment, Your Honor," Vandling said. "This is developing into a situation which I hadn't anticipated. I am afraid I have to admit that I hadn't interrogated Dr. Renault as to the cause of death because I felt certain that the presence of poison which had been found at the time of the autopsy would completely answer the question as to the cause of death."

"You'll have your opportunity on redirect examination,"

Mason said. "I'm asking the doctor specific questions now on cross-examination and I'm getting specific answers. I want to have those answers in the record."

"Well, they're in the record," Vandling said.

"Are you trying to object to my cross-examination?" Mason asked.

Vandling sat down and said, "No, go right ahead. Let's get the facts, whatever they are."

Mason said, "Now, let's get this matter straight, Doctor. You saw the man die?"

"Yes, sir."

"You are familiar with the symptoms of cyanide of potassium poisoning?"

"Yes, sir."

"And you don't think that he died from such poison?"

"I am quite certain he did not. There were none of the typical symptoms. His death was due to weakness, to shock and to an inability to recuperate from the ingestion of poison."

"*You* don't know that he took poison."

"I know what he told me and I know what his symptoms were."

"But most of the symptoms were those that he described to you, were they not?"

"Well, he described his symptoms, naturally. A doctor asks a patient those things."

"You don't *know* that he took *any* poison?"

"I know that his condition was such that it was compatible with the symptoms he had described."

"He told you that his wife was trying to poison him. He told you that he had taken a piece of candy from a box, that shortly after taking it—"

"Immediately after taking it," the doctor said.

"All right, immediately after taking it that he was seized with symptoms, with pains, cramps and vomiting."

"Yes, sir."

"And it was Davenport's opinion this was due to arsenic poisoning?"

"To poisoning. I don't think he mentioned arsenic. Yes, perhaps he did, too."

"You're the one who mentioned arsenic?"

"I may have."

"The deceased had been in Paradise for some time?"

"So he said."

"He was on his way to his home in Los Angeles?"

"Yes, sir."

"And he told you he had eaten a piece of candy and then become ill?"

"I've said that many times. Yes, sir. I think I've answered that question in one form or another repeatedly."

"But *you* don't *know* he took a piece of candy?"

"Only by what he told me."

"You don't know of your own knowledge that he took a piece of candy?"

"No, sir."

"But you do know of your own knowledge that he did *not* die of poisoning by cyanide of potassium?"

"His symptoms were not in any way similar to those I should have expected to find from such poison. No, sir."

Mason said, "Now I'll go a little further with you, Doctor. You have stated that the man described his symptoms of poisoning?"

"Yes, sir."

"And that his condition was compatible with such poisoning?"

"Yes, sir."

"And that when you left the man at somewhere around three o'clock in the afternoon he was dead?"

"Yes, sir."

"Now then, if that is the case," Mason said, *"where did he get the meal of bacon and eggs that Dr. Hoxie found in the man's stomach and which he estimated had been ingested shortly before death?"*

"Do you want my opinion?" Dr. Renault asked.

"I'm asking you."

"It is my opinion that his wife managed in some way,

after I had left her alone with him, to get him to take some food, that that food caused his death."

"In what manner?"

"I don't know. I do know that I would not have approved a meal of that sort. The man was in a condition where he should have had liquids, no solids, nothing heavy. I had actually given him some intravenous nourishment."

"How could a man who was dying from exhaustion and shock and debilitation sit up in bed and eat a meal of bacon and eggs?" Mason asked.

"I don't know, I'm sure."

"You can't account for it?"

"I can't account for it."

"Would you say that the patient was in such a condition that he couldn't have eaten bacon and eggs?"

Dr. Renault said, "There is no question but what the body on which the post-mortem was performed was that of the same man who had been my patient. I certainly would not have thought he could have eaten a meal of that sort. He undoubtedly was prevailed upon to do so. The meal was found in his stomach. Therefore he must have taken it. I simply wouldn't have believed it was possible."

"All right, let's get certain things straight," Mason said. "As a doctor you know that the man did not die of poisoning by cyanide of potassium?"

"I feel certain he did not."

"You don't know of your own knowledge that he ever ate any candy, do you?"

"Not of my own knowledge."

"You don't know of your own knowledge that he ingested any poison at all?"

"Well . . . well, I can't swear to it, of course. I wasn't there."

"For all that you know of your own knowledge, Doctor, Edward Davenport may have contracted a typical case of food poisoning. He may have attributed that to poison which had been administered by his wife, and he may have been quite mistaken."

"As far as I know of my own knowledge."

"It is a frequent occurrence, is it not, Doctor, for a man to suffer food poisoning and to think that the food may have been deliberately poisoned rather than merely contaminated?"

"I suppose so."

"Have you ever encountered such a case in your practice?"

"I—yes, I believe I have."

"And you know that Edward Davenport didn't die from cyanide of potassium poisoning?"

"I am certain he didn't."

"That's all," Mason said.

"Now just a moment," Vandling said, as Dr. Renault started to leave the stand. "I want to question you, Doctor. I have talked with you before, have I not?"

"Yes, sir."

"And at no time did you tell me that Mr. Davenport's death was not due to cyanide of potassium poisoning?"

"You didn't ask me specifically," Dr. Renault said. "I will state by way of explanation that I felt his wife had administered poison, that the poisoning had been fatal, that in my opinion the man could well have died because of the after effects of that poison or that a second dose of poison could have been administered shortly before his death. I used the word poison. I did not say cyanide of potassium and you did not ask me. I told you specifically that in my opinion the man could have died solely because his system failed to rally from the shock of the effects of poison which had been administered in a piece of candy at about seven o'clock in the morning."

"Yes, I guess you did," Vandling admitted, "but you didn't tell me specifically that he couldn't have died from cyanide poisoning."

"I wasn't asked. I see no reason to come into conflict with some other physician unless the question is asked me under such circumstances that I cannot avoid answering. Mr. Mason asked me a specific question and I gave him a specific answer. I had determined that I would give that answer if the questions were asked and I couldn't avoid it. I was with the man when he passed away. That death might have been due to some poison which acted upon the heart or it could have been due to the shock of the earlier poison, but the symptoms of death which I would have expected had cyanide of potassium been administered were not present, not at that time.''

''You know how much cyanide was found in the man's stomach at the time of the autopsy?''

''I do.''

''And that was an amount sufficient to cause death?''

''Very definitely.''

''So that—now wait,'' Vandling said. ''If the man hadn't died from cyanide poisoning he would have died from cyanide poisoning. I mean that he had enough cyanide in his system to have killed him even if you don't think he died from cyanide poisoning.''

''I object to the question,'' Mason said, ''as being argumentative, as not being proper cross-examination, and as being completely ambiguous. The question is not what the man would have died from if he hadn't died from something else. It's a question of what caused his death.''

''I think so,'' Judge Siler said. ''I'll sustain the objection to the question in that form.''

Vandling said, ''Your Honor, this is a most peculiar situation. Dr. Hoxie is a very competent physician and toxicologist. He has testified to finding enough poison in the stomach of the dead man to have caused his death. He specifically names that poison as cyanide of potassium, a very quick-acting, fatal poison. Dr. Renault now offers it as his opinion that the man did not die from cyanide poisoning. It is, of course, only his opinion.''

''He is a physician. He has given his opinion,'' Judge Siler said.

''And he was *your* witness,'' Mason added.

''Your Honor,'' Vandling said, ''I think under the circumstances the prosecution is justified in asking a continuance of this matter.

''I will state frankly that at this time the dismissal of proceedings in this case would not constitute a bar to a further prosecution. I could dismiss this complaint right now and arrest this woman on the same charge tomorrow.''

''Why don't you do it?'' Mason asked.

''I'm not ready to do it yet. I want to investigate the case a little further. I may state, Your Honor, that in a sense I am bound by the fact that Dr. Renault is my witness. If I had simply placed Dr. Hoxie on the stand and shown the cause of death by the autopsy, if I had shown the presence of poison in the candy and the fingerprints of the defendant upon that candy, particularly after she had stated that she had never opened the box of candy, I would have established a *prima facie* case.''

''Do you want to ask me to bind the defendant over on the evidence in the case as it *now* stands?'' Judge Siler asked.

''I don't know, Your Honor,'' Vandling said. ''The situation is somewhat complicated. The record now shows that Dr. Renault was called as my witness and that he has now stated positively that in his opinion the man did not die from poisoning by cyanide.''

''And,'' Mason pointed out, ''your own doctor couldn't find any evidence of chocolate candy in the stomach of the decedent.''

''I would like to withdraw Dr. Renault from the stand and ask Dr. Hoxie to return, and ask him one question,'' Vandling said.

''Is there any objection?'' Judge Siler asked.

Mason smiled. ''No objection, Your Honor.''

''Step down, Dr. Renault, if you will, please. Dr. Hoxie, will you come forward? You have already been sworn, Doctor. I just want to ask you a question.''

Dr. Hoxie marched up to the witness stand. He was bristling with professional indignation.

''You have heard Dr. Renault's testimony?'' Vandling said.

''I have,'' Dr. Hoxie snapped.

''Do you have any doubt as to the cause of death in this case?''

''None whatever. The man whom I autopsied died of poisoning by cyanide of potassium.''

"That is, there was enough cyanide of potassium in his stomach to have caused death?"

"Yes, sir."

"Now I'm going to ask you another question. It's rather farfetched and it may be rather gruesome. Would it be possible for a person to pump out the stomach of a cadaver?"

"Why, certainly."

"All right. Would it be possible for a person to pump something else into the stomach of the cadaver?"

Dr. Hoxie hesitated. "Are you asking me now," he said at length, "whether I think that that could have been done in this case?"

"I'm asking you as to a general possibility."

"I presume it's possible generally. I will state, however, that in my opinion Edward Davenport died of the effects of cyanide of potassium. Not only was the poison present, but there were symptoms present, the evidence of froth, the characteristic odor, the general symptoms. In my opinion the man died almost immediately after ingesting a very large dose of cyanide of potassium. He had been drinking for an hour or so before his death. He had also eaten bacon and eggs an hour or so before his death."

Vandling explained to Judge Siler, "I am trying, Your Honor, to get at the facts in this case. I want to get a solution of a seemingly contradictory situation."

"There's nothing contradictory as far as I am concerned," Dr. Hoxie said. "In my opinion the man died of poisoning by cyanide of potassium. The conditions were all there. The poison was there. The man simply couldn't have lived after having ingested the amount of poison that I found in his stomach. All of the conditions of cyanic poisoning were present. In my opinion it was the cause of death, regardless of what anyone else may say to the contrary."

"Do you have any further questions or cross-examination?" Vandling asked Mason.

"Do you think the poison was ingested in a piece of candy?" Mason asked.

"I do not."

"Would you say it was not?"

"I would say that I don't think the poison was taken in candy. I think death was very rapid and I found no evidence of candy although I tried very carefully to find candy in the stomach content."

"How do you think the poison was taken?"

"I don't think it was taken in food. It may have been administered in whisky. There was whisky in the stomach and alcohol in the blood. I have one other theory which is a possibility which I don't care to state."

Mason thought that over, then said, "Is that theory that the dead man could have been given a straight dose of poison—let us say as a medicine?"

"Yes."

"That's all, Doctor," Mason said, smiling.

"Just one question on redirect, Doctor," Vandling said triumphantly. "Then, in your opinion, it is possible the defendant could have given Edward Davenport this poison under the guise of medicine?"

"No."

"What? I thought you just said the cyanide could have been given as medicine."

"I did, but not by Mrs. Davenport, because she wasn't in the room within the necessary time limit. My opinion is that Edward Davenport lived less than two minutes after ingesting that poison."

"Any more questions on cross-examination?" Vandling asked Mason.

"None whatsoever," Mason said. "You're doing fine. Go right ahead. It's your omelette. Try to unscramble it."

"I'd like to ask for a continuance," Vandling said. "It is past the noon hour now, Your Honor. Court usually adjourns until two o'clock. I am going to ask the Court to adjourn until four o'clock this afternoon."

"Does the defense have any objections?" Judge Siler asked.

"I think not, under the circumstances," Mason said. "In fact we'll grant a continuance until tomorrow morning at ten o'clock if the prosecution wishes."

"I should like to have such a continuance provided it is

stipulated that . . . I would prefer to have the motion come from the defendant,'' Vandling said.

"I'll make such a motion," Mason said promptly.

"Very well," Judge Siler ruled. "On the motion of the defendant the case is continued until tomorrow morning at ten o'clock. The defendant will remain in custody. Court's adjourned."

Vandling looked across at Mason. "Well," he said, "I had been warned to expect the unexpected in dealing with you, but this is the damnedest thing I've ever encountered in all my career."

Mason smiled. "What are you going to do?"

"I don't know," Vandling said. "I can get her bound over, but in view of the testimony of Dr. Renault I'd have a hell of a time getting her convicted in front of a jury."

"Well, at least you're frank," Mason told him.

"There's no use trying to cover things up with you," Vandling said. "You know as well as I do what would happen if a situation like this developed in front of a jury."

"Are you going to dismiss the case?"

"I don't think so. I walked into this thing with my eyes shut. I think probably I can put on a case before a jury without calling Dr. Renault, and force you to call him as your witness."

"And then what?" Mason asked.

"Then," Vandling said, lowering his voice, "I'd attack his professional competency. I don't think he's too highly regarded in medical circles here. He's drifted around. He's a mature man, yet he's only practiced in Crampton for three years. I believe he was in trouble over narcotics at one time. That's why Dr. Hoxie became so indignant at the idea of his findings being questioned by a man who had no more professional standing than Dr. Renault."

"Dr. Renault seemed positive enough," Mason said.

"He sure was positive enough."

"And then, of course," Mason went on, "you have the spectacle of the corpse climbing out of the window."

Vandling frowned. "It's a strange case. Someone might have pushed the corpse through the window, then impersonated the dead man. I asked for a continuance because I have a plan in mind. You might be surprised if you knew what I was thinking right now.''

"I may not know what you're thinking," Mason said, "but I'll bet five dollars I know what you're going to do."

"What?''

"You're going to call the district attorney of Los Angeles County and suggest that there are a few technical matters that are bothering you in this case up here, and that under the circumstances you think it would be better to have the Los Angeles grand jury indict Myrna Davenport for the murder of Hortense Paxton and try her down there on that charge first.''

Vandling threw back his head and laughed. "Well," he said, "I'd been warned that you'd anticipate my every move. Well, if you'll excuse me, I'll go telephone.''

As Vandling walked away, Mason turned to the officer. "Just a moment, I want to confer with my client before you take her back to jail.''

He took Mrs. Davenport's arm, took her over to a deserted corner of the courtroom and said, "What was this you were telling me, that you had never opened that box of candy?''

"Mr. Mason, I'm telling you the truth. I never opened that box of candy.''

"Your fingerprints got on the candy," Mason said.

"There's something wrong. Those can't be my fingerprints. They have been forged in some way.''

Mason said, "The question of forged fingerprints comes up every once in a while, but so far as I know there's never been a case on record where a jury has held that a defendant's fingerprints were successfully forged. Not when the fingerprints were left in place. When they have been lifted there's another angle to the case. These prints are in place.''

Myrna Davis lowered her eyes. "Well," she said in her low voice, "those aren't my fingerprints. They can't be.''

"Because you didn't open the box of candy?''

"Because I didn't open the box of candy.''

Sara Ansel came bustling forward from the back of the courtroom where she had been seated as a spectator.

"Mr. Mason," she said, "may I talk with you?"

Mason nodded.

She pushed her way through the swinging gate and entered the railed enclosure reserved for officers of the court.

"Mr. Mason, I know, I absolutely know that Myrna didn't do any of those things they claim she did. She didn't feed Ed Davenport any bacon and eggs. He didn't eat a thing while we were there. He was barely conscious and could hardly talk and she didn't enter that room after Dr. Renault had left. She—"

Myrna looked coldly at Sara Ansel. "Go away," she said.

Sara Ansel said, "Myrna, my dear, I'm trying to help you."

"You've done everything you could to betray me," she said.

"Myrna, do you realize what you're saying?"

"Of course I do."

Sara Ansel said, "You can't. You're upset and excited. Now, Myrna, dear, I know how your prints got on the candy. You gave Ed a full box, all right. You put it in his suitcase. But there was another partially filled box in the living room. You and I had been eating candy. There were two boxes in the living room, both partially empty. You consolidated those two partially empty boxes. So your fingerprints were on some of those candies you handled. Ed must have taken that box you consolidated as well as the one you packed in his suitcase.

"Then while he was in Paradise he must have eaten that fresh box you had put in his suitcase. That left the other box in his suitcase—the one you had consolidated from the two partially empty boxes.

"I'm almost certain that box the officers have now is the one you fixed up from the two open boxes. I could *almost* swear to it."

Without a word to Sara Ansel, Myrna turned to the officer. "Will you please take me back to jail?" she said. "I'm tired."

The officer led Myrna Davenport away. Sara Ansel turned to Mason and said angrily, "*Well*, can you beat *that*! Here I try to be of some help to her and I get slapped down like that.''

''Well,'' Mason said, ''you have to admit that you tried to do everything you could to help the Los Angeles authorities make a case against her.''

''That was when I was excited and—the poor child. She never harmed a fly. I am sorry. I am terribly sorry for what I did, Mr. Mason, but I'm certainly not going to go around turning the other cheek to that mousy little nincompoop. Why, if it hadn't been for me Ed Davenport would have robbed her blind. He'd have had her funds so involved she wouldn't have had a cent in the world except what he was willing to give her, and then he'd have left her. I know it just as well as I know anything. I've been around men enough to know them.''

''Are you going to be here for a while?'' Mason asked.

''Certainly. You heard what the judge said. I've got to be here.''

''I may want to talk with you,'' Mason told her.

''Well, you'll find me at the Hotel Fresno.''

''Thanks, you may be seeing me. I may want to ask you some more questions—about the candy.''

Chapter 12

Perry Mason, Paul Drake and Della Street gathered in Mason's suite in the Californian Hotel.

"Well," Mason said, "we're at least getting the situation clarified."

"Clarified!" Paul Drake exclaimed. "It's mixed up until I can't make head or tail of it and I doubt if anyone else can."

"Why, Paul!" Mason said. "As it now stands there's only one person in the world who could have murdered Edward Davenport."

"You mean Myrna?" Drake asked.

Mason smiled. "How would Myrna have gone about murdering him?"

"That's easy," Drake said. "After she arrived in Crampton she could have given him a dose of cyanide of potassium, then called Dr. Renault to come down on an emergency."

"Then how would she have removed the body?"

"By having some male accomplice slide the body out of the window and then put on the red-spotted pajamas and jump out when he was certain a witness was watching—a witness who was far enough away so he could see the man's figure but couldn't see his face."

"Very interesting," Mason said. "But how would she have known that her husband was going to get sick when he reached Crampton?"

"She didn't care when he got sick," Drake said. "She was an opportunist. She simply administered the poison because she found him sick. She wouldn't have cared whether he'd been taken sick in Crampton, Fresno, Bakersfield, Paradise or Timbuktu."

"That's fine," Mason said. "But you're overlooking the

grave. How did Mrs. Davenport know there was a grave waiting out there three miles out of town?''

''Because she'd dug it.''

''When?''

''She'd probably gone up the week before and dug the grave, or else had her male accomplice do it.''

''Then,'' Mason said, ''she must have known he was going to get sick at the exact moment he reached Crampton.''

Drake started scratching his head. ''Well I'll be damned,'' he said.

''Who did murder him?'' Della Street asked.

''Someone who knew that he was going to be sick when he reached Crampton,'' Mason said.

''But who could that have been?''

Mason said, ''I have an idea but it's going to take a little checking. As nearly as I can tell only one person was in a position to know what was going to happen.''

''Who?'' Della Street asked.

Mason said, ''I won't make any predictions at present. We'll go out and look for some additional evidence while our friend, Talbert Vandling, is having an argument with the district attorney in Los Angeles.''

''An argument?'' Drake asked.

''Sure,'' Mason said. ''Don't think the district attorney of Los Angeles is going to be anxious to take over now.''

''Why not?''

''Because Fresno started in on the case. It made a pass at convicting Myrna Davenport and then suddenly backed up when it found the facts were all cockeyed.

''If the district attorney of Los Angeles could have had her convicted of any crime in Fresno, even the crime of being an accessory after the fact, or of having negligently administered poison, he'd have been only too glad to have prosecuted her for the murder of Hortense Paxton. Then when she took the stand he'd have impeached her by showing she'd been convicted of a felony and shown what the felony was. After that she wouldn't have stood a ghost of a chance.

''As it is now the district attorney in Los Angeles can show that Hortense Paxton died from poison, that Myrna Davenport was in a position to benefit by her death, that Myrna Davenport had some poison in the house and that she tried to conceal that poison after it was learned that the body of Hortense Paxton was being exhumed.''

"It's a strong case," Drake said.

"It's a strong case but it's not a convicting case," Mason replied. "Just one or two additional facts and they'd be sure of a conviction. On the other hand, just one or two little additional facts in favor of the defense and the best they could hope for would be a hung jury."

"What facts could you get in favor of the defense?"

Mason grinned. "The poisoning of Ed Davenport."

"How do you mean?"

"The person who poisoned him would presumably be the person who poisoned Hortense Paxton."

"Could you bring that in?" Drake asked.

"Under other circumstances the district attorney would try to one way or another. If he thought Myrna Davenport could be shown to be guilty, he'd use the old dodge of showing that these were crimes of a similar pattern and all of that. As it is now, the defense would claim it was entitled to bring the facts in in the same way. At least the defense could try to bring them in and if the prosecution fought to keep these facts out the jury would become so suspicious of the whole thing that it wouldn't convict.''

"Well," Drake said, "that means that the D.A. in Los Angeles will tell Vandling that he started this thing and to go ahead and finish it."

Mason nodded.

"So what will Vandling do?" Drake asked.

"Try to get some additional evidence. If he doesn't he'll have to dismiss."

"Why?"

"Look at it in this way," Mason said. "Myrna Davenport put candy in her husband's bag. The candy was poisoned. It contained arsenic and cyanide of potassium. Dr. Renault can swear the man told him he had symptoms of arsenic poisoning but he didn't die of cyanide of potassium. He can't swear of his own knowledge that the man had any symptoms of arsenic poisoning. He only knows that from what Davenport told him, and that's hearsay and not admissible.

"Dr. Hoxie will swear that the man must have died from cyanide of potassium poisoning but he can't find any trace of candy in the stomach. Therefore he couldn't have died from eating poisoned candy. The only thing they can really connect Myrna Davenport with is the poisoned candy."

"So what do we do?" Drake asked.

"We drive out to the site of the grave up near Crampton," Mason said, "and we look for something."

"For what?"

"Where a six-wheeled vehicle has been parked."

"A six-wheeled vehicle?" Drake asked.

"That's right."

"What do you mean?"

"A four-wheeled automobile and a two-wheeled house trailer."

"I don't get it," Drake said.

"And then," Mason went on, "we try to find Mabel Norge."

"Why?"

"Because we want to question her."

"How do we go about looking for her?"

Mason said, "You have her description. Tall, brunette, twenty-seven or twenty-eight; well-formed but not heavy; slate-gray eyes; narrow, black, penciled eyebrows. In order to find her you go to San Bernardino and start looking through the hotels and the motels. You also have someone keep in touch with the district attorney in Butte County or try to get a line into his office."

"How come?"

"I think she'll be communicating with him."

"Why? What gives you that idea?"

"Because she doesn't want to be a fugitive and she doesn't want to have her absence misconstrued. I think probably she'll telephone the district attorney and tell him where he can reach her but ask him to keep the address confidential."

"You think the D.A. in Butte County will protect her?" Drake asked.

"I think he'll try to."

"Why?"

"Because he'll use her either as a red herring or an ace-in-the-hole, depending on which will better suit his purpose, and if he alone knows where she is it strengthens his hand."

"Okay, Perry." Drake sighed. "What do you want me to do now?"

"Right at the moment," Mason said, "get your men covering San Bernardino. I want to find Mabel Norge. I'm particularly anxious not to disturb her complacency. My best guess is that she's telephoned or will telephone the D.A. at Butte County. He'll tell her to stay where she is. I don't want anyone to know that we're looking for her. It shouldn't be too difficult a job. People who go to motels are usually transients. They're there for one day. A young, attractive woman who stays over for a longer period should attract attention."

"Okay. What next?"

"Della and I are going out to the location of the grave. We're going to look around. We should be back shortly after you have this San Bernardino angle covered."

"What about Sara Ansel?" Drake asked. "She's been pestering me, trying to see me, trying to explain that she's Myrna's good friend and that she wants to patch everything up."

"Leave her alone," Mason said. "Leave her severely alone, Paul."

"That's all very well," Drake retorted, grinning, "but how am I going to get her to leave me alone?"

"Probably," Mason said, "you'll have to club her over the head. Come on, Della, let's go."

Mason and Della Street left the hotel, drove to Crampton, then turned off on the road, which had been indicated in the maps shown by Vandling, to the location of the grave.

Quite a few curiosity seekers had been on the ground. There were evidences of cars having been parked. Empty film containers bore mute testimony to the amount of amateur photography that had taken place. Dozens of feet had tramped the ground around the shallow grave.

Mason said, "Della, if my theory is correct, there was a

car with a house trailer parked within a very short distance. It probably was here for two or three days. I'd like to find where it stayed."

Della Street raised her eyebrows. "If your theory is correct?"

"That's right."

"And what, may I ask, is your theory?"

Mason said, "Come, come, Della. Don't deprive me of my triumph."

"What do you mean?"

"If it turns out I'm right," Mason said, "I will point out to Paul Drake the simple, elemental steps of reasoning that made it absolutely imperative that certain events should have happened in a certain sequence."

"And if you're wrong?"

"If I'm wrong," Mason said, "and I don't give you my theory in advance, I can say casually, 'Well, I had a theory but that theory doesn't seem to be borne out by the facts so I won't waste your time mentioning it.' "

"That's all right for you to say to Paul Drake," Della Street said, "but aren't you going to put me on a little different footing?"

"That's exactly it," Mason said. "I want to make an even better impression on you than I do on Paul Drake."

"You don't have to. You have already made it."

"After all, Della, you wouldn't expect a magician to tell you how he expected to perform the trick before he performed it. It would take away all of the glamour and all of the mystery."

"You can't take away any of your glamour by taking away the mystery," Della Street said, "but if you want me to cooperate, tramping around through this country looking for a place where a house trailer parked, you'd better tell me why."

"Let's look at it this way, Della. The whole scheme of murder depended on the fact that someone must have known that Edward Davenport was going to be taken seriously ill immediately after leaving Fresno, that by the time he had driven to Crampton he would be so sick he couldn't possibly continue his journey. He would have to move into a motel

180

and call a doctor. Otherwise, there couldn't have been any murder. There couldn't have been any planning for a murder, at least to the extent of having a grave all ready."

"That's true. You've said that before, Chief."

"Well," Mason said, "who was the person? Who was the *one* person who could have known that Davenport would be taken sick at that particular place at that particular time?"

"Mabel Norge, the secretary?" Della Street ventured.

Mason laughed. "I've given you all the clues I'm going to, Della. You go look for the place where the house trailer was parked over on the east side of this hill. I'll look over on the west side. But don't go far. Don't get out of the sound of my voice. It should be around here within a hundred and fifty or two hundred yards. If you see anyone or if you think you're being watched, don't be afraid to let out a whoop. I'll be listening."

Della Street hesitated a moment. "I get no more clues?"

"Not unless you find them," Mason said. "After all, if I pull a rabbit out of the hat I don't want to have the audience yawn in my face. I'm enjoying myself tremendously, Della."

"You're being a prig," she said and, turning, walked down the hill and into the patch of brush.

Mason waited a few seconds, then went down on the other side, walking slowly in long zigzags, looking for wheel tracks.

Fifteen minutes later Mason was back on the hill, whistling for Della Street.

For a few anxious moments he waited, then was just starting down the hill when he heard her call some distance away.

Mason whistled once more, then hurried through the brush. At length he picked up Della Street's tracks, and, whistling again, once more heard her call.

Again Mason walked a distance of some fifty yards, again he whistled and again received an answer.

"Heavens, Della," he said, "I didn't want you to go so far away. What would have happened if you'd met some—"

"I'm on a hot trail," she said.

Mason hurried up to her and Della Street pointed to automobile tracks in the soft ground.

"Oh-oh," Mason said.

"They're narrow jeep tracks," Della said. "Does that mean anything?"

"It may."

"Would that eliminate the necessity of a house trailer?"

"I don't know," Mason said. "I think not. Let's follow the tracks."

"Which direction?"

"Where did you pick them up, Della?"

"Within—oh, I don't know—a hundred feet of the hill, I guess."

"All right, let's follow them away from the hill then."

Mason and Della Street followed the tracks for a hundred yards, then suddenly came to a little clearing in the brush where a rather vague but quite passable roadway led out toward the highway. Here there was a cleared space where it was evident that a house trailer had been parked. Not only were the tracks visible but there was a little hole in the ground, washed by drain water from a sink just back of the left wheel.

Della Street made a little bow. "Very well, Mr. Mason," she said, "you have now pulled the rabbit out of the hat. You have found the location of the house trailer. Now what do we do?"

"Now," Mason said, "we carefully mark the place. We go back to Fresno. We have Paul Drake get a couple of his most trusted and observant men and we have them come out here and go over this place with a fine-toothed comb, listing every article."

"Article?" Della Street asked.

Mason pointed to a small pile of empty tin cans.

"Everything," he said. "Every single article. We want a complete inventory of this spot before anything happens to it."

"Can't we take the inventory while we're here?"

"We have other work to do," Mason told her. "We'll be starting for San Bernardino within the next hour."

"But after you've duly dazzled everyone by pulling the

rabbit out of the hat, will you tell us how you knew the rabbit was in the hat?'' Della Street asked.

Mason said, ''You haven't answered my question yet, Della.''

''What question?''

''Who was the person? Who was the one person who could possibly have known that Edward Davenport was going to leave Fresno at around seven o'clock in the morning, that he was going to be taken violently ill as soon as he started driving, and that by the time he reached Crampton he would be so completely ill that he wouldn't be able to go on, that he'd have to go to bed and call for a doctor?''

''There just wasn't any such person,'' Della Street said. ''There couldn't have been.''

''Then it couldn't have been premeditated murder.''

''But it had to be, otherwise—why, Chief, the grave was dug two or three days in advance. It's the most cold-blooded, diabolical crime you can think of. That is, if that grave was intended all along for Ed Davenport.''

''It was,'' Mason told her. ''Come on, Della. We're going back to Fresno. We're going to charter a plane to take us to San Bernardino. By the time we get there Drake's men should have located Mabel Norge.''

''And if they haven't?''

''If they haven't we'll try locating her ourselves, but I think they'll have her spotted. In the meantime we'll have Drake's men get busy and cover every inch of the ground out here, looking for clues. For instance, Della, notice these cans. Now here's a can that held baked beans. It was opened smoothly with one of those can openers that cuts around the rim of the can, leaving the edges nice and smooth and taking the top all the way off. Notice the inside of the can.''

''What about it?''

''The remnants of the beans are dried and hard.''

''Meaning that the can has been there for some time?''

''A week or ten days probably.''

''Very well, Mr. Magician,'' she told him. ''I know my place. I'm supposed to put on very short skirts and tights and stand bowing and smiling and looking awed while you pull the rabbit out of the hat. I believe that's the function of the magician's assistant, isn't it?''

''That's right,'' Mason said. ''Her gams distract the attention of the audience.''

''But not of the magician?'' Della Street asked lightly.

''Sometimes even the magician,'' Mason conceded.

Chapter 13

The sun was low as Mason's chartered plane droned over the high plateau country.

Down below the desert stretched interminably. The tall, weird shapes of the Joshua palms cast long, angular shadows. Over on the right snow-capped mountains turned to a rosy glow in the rays of the setting sun. Then the desert gave way to mountains, piling up in jagged, tumbled peaks until the crests became covered with dark green pines. A lake flashed into view, bordered by many sumptuous houses. A paved road ran around the lake. Buildings were scattered through the dense pines.

Abruptly the whole country seemed to drop away and far below in the valley San Bernardino clustered in an orderly array of straight thoroughfares and houses which seemed to have been carved from miniature sugar lumps topped with pink roofs and then viewed through the wrong end of a telescope.

The plane tilted sharply.

"It'll be a few miles to town from the airport where I want to land," the pilot explained.

"That's all right," Mason said. "We'll rent a car."

Lights came on in the valley below. The pilot skimmed over orange groves and prosperous ranches, then taxied the plane into a landing.

"I can't fly you back tonight," he said. "I'm not licensed for night flights."

"Never mind," Mason told him. "We'll get back, don't bother about us."

Mason paid off the aviator, and took a taxicab to a place where he could rent a car, then rang the number Paul Drake had given him and explained who he was.

"You're in luck," the operative told him. "We located your party just about twenty minutes ago."

"Where is she?"

"Staying at the Antlers Hotel, and this is one for the book."

"What's that?"

"She's registered under the name of Mabel Davenport."

"That's fine," Mason said. "You have her under surveillance?"

"Yes. She's been out most of the afternoon. She came in shortly after we had her located and she's in her room now."

"You have a man on duty there?"

"Yes."

"How will I know him?"

"He's wearing a gray suit, about thirty-five years old, five feet ten and a half, a hundred and seventy pounds, with a blue and red necktie and a gold horseshoe tiepin."

"Okay," Mason said. "He's expecting us?"

"He'll be expecting you. He'll be in touch with me within the next few minutes and I'll tell him you're coming."

"That's fine," Mason said, and hung up. "Well, Della, we've got our party located. She's at the Antlers Hotel, registered under the name of Mabel Davenport."

"And that's Mabel Norge, the secretary?"

Mason nodded.

"The only person," Della said, "who could possibly have known that Ed Davenport was going to be taken sick shortly after leaving Fresno."

"And how would she have known that?" Mason asked.

"Do I have to spell it out for you? She drove down to Fresno with him. She spent the night in the motel. Just before he left in the morning she saw that he took something that would make him violently ill and—"

"But he didn't register a woman with him," Mason said. "If a woman had been spending the night he'd have registered as Frank L. Stanton and wife. He was alone when he drove up and he—"

"And he had a visitor," Della Street said.

"Exactly."

"And after this visitor left, Mabel Norge joined him. She'd been waiting."

"And you think she poisoned him?"

"That's the part I can't understand. She must have given him something that made him sick."

"Just as he was leaving?"

"Just as he was leaving in the morning."

"Under those circumstances," Mason said, "he would have been as apt to have turned back and called for a doctor from Fresno as to have gone on and become sick in Crampton where the grave was so conveniently waiting."

She sighed. "I suppose you'll tell me in your own good time."

"I'll tell you as soon as I know, Della, but right now I have a theory—and that's all."

"Well, don't be such a clam. According to your theory there was only one person who knew he was to be taken sick as soon as he left Fresno and that he'd get as far as Crampton and then stop. It wasn't—good heavens, you don't mean it was Ed Davenport himself?"

"That's right."

"But why on earth? Why would he want—?"

Mason said, "We'll know some of the answers in a few minutes if Mabel Norge talks, and under the circumstances I rather think she will. It's going to be rather embarrassing to her when we step in and find her registered as Mabel Davenport."

"And you mean that Ed Davenport deliberately planned to get sick so that—?"

"Ed Davenport was the only person on earth who could have known definitely, positively and absolutely that he was going to get sick in Crampton—that is, Della, if it was planned out in advance."

"Well, it had to be planned out because of the grave."

"That at least is the theory of the prosecution," Mason said.

Della Street was silent for a few moments, trying to figure it out, then she shook her head and said, "It's too deep for me."

"I think," Mason told her, "we're going to get some information that will enable us to unravel the puzzle. Remember that telephone call we received in Paradise, Della. The man didn't ask for any kind of identification. As soon as you said hello he gave you the information about the motel in San Bernardino, then hung up."

"I get it," Della Street said, "and Mabel Norge came by the place in Paradise not simply because she was driving by but because she was waiting for a phone call that would tell her where to go."

"That's right."

"And because she didn't get that phone call she didn't know where to go and—but she knew it was somewhere in San Bernardino, and so she went to San Bernardino and waited."

"That's right."

"But why didn't she go back to the place in Paradise after we had left and—?"

"She probably did," Mason said. "She went back there and sat waiting for a telephone call that didn't come. The reason it didn't come was because you had taken the telephone call earlier. There had probably been some alternate instructions. If Mabel hadn't received the call by a certain time, say midnight, then she was to go to San Bernardino, register at the Antlers Hotel as Mabel Davenport, and await instructions there."

"But how would that account for her having embezzled money out of—?"

"Who said she embezzled money?" Mason asked.

"Well, she drew out virtually everything there was in the account in Paradise, and then disappeared."

"Exactly," Mason said. "That's not embezzlement."

"Well, it looks like it to me."

"We'll see what Mabel Norge has to say about it," Mason said.

He parked the car at the parking lot by the Antlers Hotel, entered the lobby, and had no difficulty identifying the man in the gray suit with the blue and red tie.

The man, who had been lounging by the cigar counter,

sauntered over to Mason and said, "She's in the café. She just went in for dinner. Do you know her when you see her?"

Mason nodded.

"Do you want to wait until she comes out or—?"

"No," Mason said, smiling. "We'll join her for dinner."

"Okay, you want me to stay on the job?"

"I think so," Mason said. "Come on, Della, we'll drop in on Mabel."

"She's in the second booth to the right, sitting alone," the detective said.

"Okay, we'll join her."

Mason held the swinging door open for Della Street. They entered the restaurant, turned to the right. Abruptly Mason paused, said, "Well, well, Della, here's someone we know."

Mabel Norge, who had been studying the menu, glanced up curiously and then suddenly panic filled her eyes.

"Good evening," she said coldly.

Mason moved over and extended his hand. "Well, well, Miss Norge! How are you tonight? I heard you were here."

"*You* heard I was here?" she asked after hesitating a moment in extending her hand.

"Why, yes," Mason said. "You notified the authorities in Butte County, didn't you?"

Her face colored. "They weren't supposed to tell anyone."

Mason easily and quite naturally seated himself opposite her, and Della Street slid in beside him.

"Well," Mason said, "it's nice finding you here where we can talk and—"

"I don't care to talk."

"Then it may be necessary to notify the newspapers after all, Della," Mason said to Della Street.

"The newspapers?" Mabel Norge echoed.

"Why certainly," Mason said. "You haven't kept abreast of developments up in your part of the country. You're a young woman who is very much sought after."

She bit her lip and said suddenly, "Mr. Mason, I have nothing to discuss with you. I came in here to eat. I don't care to be disturbed."

"Okay by me," Mason said. "Della, call the newspaper here. Find out who is the representative of the AP and who represents the UP. We'll get the wire services to work on this angle—"

"Mr. Mason, I told you I didn't care to be disturbed."

"It isn't what one wants in a murder case," Mason said, "particularly when the newspapers get started."

"But I have nothing to do with any murder case."

"You probably think that," Mason said, "but the facts indicate the opposite."

"There are no facts indicating the opposite. I did what I did on the definite instructions of my employer."

"Sure," Mason said, "but the definite instructions of your employer now are going to become evidence in the case."

"Mr. Halder told me it would be all right," Mabel Norge said.

Mason laughed, said, "Halder is very much on the periphery. He doesn't even know what's going on. Now Mr. Vandling is the district attorney at Fresno. He's the one who's trying the case. You ring *him* up and see what he has to say."

Mabel Norge was silent.

"She evidently doubts my word, Della," Mason said. "There's a telephone booth down by the cashier's cage. Get Vandling on the line. Tell him that Mabel Norge is here registered under an assumed name and ask him what he wants to do about it. Perhaps it's better to let him work through the local police and then the newspapermen can pick the thing up from the local police."

Della Street arose.

"Got plenty of quarters?" Mason asked.

"I can get some at the cashier's cage."

"Well, that's fine," Mason said. "Get him and—"

"Don't," Mabel Norge said, and suddenly began to cry.

"Now wait, wait," Mason said. "We don't want to upset you, Miss Norge, but, good Lord, you can see the plain implications of the case. You know what Mr. Vandling will do. He finds you here registered under the name of Mabel Davenport, so it's quite natural to assume that you were to

190

join Mr. Davenport here, or, rather, that he was to join you, as Mr. and Mrs. Davenport—''

''How dare you say a thing like that?''

''Why, your own conduct—good Lord, you don't think there's any other interpretation that the press would place upon it, do you?''

''If the press intimates anything like that I'll . . . I'll sue them.''

''Sure,'' Mason said. ''You can sue but what good would that do? You get up in front of a jury and some attorney starts examining you, you have to admit that you disappeared from Paradise, that you looted the Paradise bank account before you left, that you came down here and registered under the name of Mabel Davenport, and that you were waiting for Ed Davenport to join you.''

''You forget that I knew he was dead before I left Paradise.''

''No, you felt that he wasn't dead.''

''What gives you any grounds for saying that?''

''Come, come,'' Mason said. ''Now let's be grownup. Della, I guess Miss Norge doesn't realize what we know.''

''Well,'' Mabel Norge said, ''what *do* you know?''

Mason said, ''Now let's see. You were supposed to make some deposits on Monday. Then you were supposed to draw virtually all of the cash out of the account and you were to be at the office that night, awaiting a telephone call. That telephone call was to tell you where to take the money. It was to be someplace here in San Bernardino. In the event you didn't get the telephone call by a certain hour you were to come to San Bernardino, register at the Antlers Hotel here under the name of Mabel Davenport and await instructions.''

''I don't know how you know all this,'' Mabel Norge said.

''Well,'' Mason said, ''those are the facts. Why try to deny them?''

''Those aren't the facts, that is, that's not *exactly* the way it happened.''

''It's close enough to it,'' Mason said, ''so that I know what to tell the district attorney at Fresno and how the newspapers will write it up. Of course, they'll adopt the attitude that you were Ed Davenport's mistress, that he wanted to get a lot of cash together and disappear with you.''

''Why, that's absurd, that's utterly ridiculous. That's absolutely libelous, Mr. Mason. I can never—why—he had a mining deal that he wanted to put across and he had to have a large sum of cash. I don't have to talk to you.''

''That's right,'' Mason said, ''but what are you going to do now? You're in a very peculiar position. If you take any of that money and use it for yourself you're guilty of embezzlement. If you return to Paradise you'll be questioned as to where you went and what you did and why. You've got to tell your story sooner or later. If you're picked up here under the name of Mabel Davenport with Ed Davenport's cash in your possession it looks as though you have been caught in the act of embezzling money.''

''Well, I didn't embezzle any money,'' she said, ''and I know exactly what I'm doing. I've had the assurance of the district attorney at Oroville that everything I do is all right, and I'm going to call him and tell him I don't want to be annoyed.''

Mason nodded to Della Street. ''This time, Della,'' he said, ''I'm not bluffing. I'll call Vandling myself.''

Mason and Della Street left the table. Mason walked down to the cashier's desk, secured some quarters, went to the telephone booth and Mason called Vandling at Fresno.

''Hello,'' Mason said when he had Vandling on the line. ''This is Mason. How's your case coming?''

''Our case you mean.''

''Don't tie me up with it,'' Mason said, laughing. ''Are you going to dismiss?''

''Well,'' Vandling said, ''I still haven't made up my mind as to what I'm going to do, but Los Angeles says it doesn't want to pull my chestnuts out of the fire for me. I started the thing and I seem to be stuck with it. I can get the defendant bound over for trial all right. I may have to dismiss and start a new preliminary. That'll give me time to think and perhaps turn up some new evidence.''

"That's fine," Mason told him. "Perhaps I can turn up some new evidence. Mabel Norge, the secretary to Edward Davenport, was instructed to make some last-minute deposits and then draw out everything in the Paradise account. She's here at the Antlers Hotel in San Bernardino registered under the name of Mabel Davenport. She'd have quite a story to tell if you grabbed her as a material witness. She won't talk voluntarily and she's getting ready to skip out.

"It may interest you to know that she's told a part of her story to the district attorney at Oroville and he gave her his official blessing. She thinks she's sitting pretty. But she didn't tell him the whole story. If she tells it to you it may help."

"What are you trying to do? Make a case against your client?" Vandling asked.

"I'm trying to make a case against the murderer," Mason replied. "Perhaps we can walk into court tomorrow morning and clarify the situation."

"You slay me," Vandling said. "In other words, Mason, I fear the Greeks when they're bearing gifts."

"No," Mason said, "it's an unfortunate trait of human nature. You accept all kinds of phony tips from touts and never win, then some day a quiet, sedate individual comes along with a straight tip on a dark horse in the fifth race and you pass it up because you're too smart to fall for any more of that stuff. After the fifth race you kick yourself all over the lot."

Mason abruptly hung up the telephone.

"Mabel Norge left the restaurant hurriedly," Della Street reported.

"That's fine," Mason said, grinning. "If she resorts to flight, it will look like the devil."

"And if she doesn't?" Della Street asked.

"If she doesn't, Vandling will get her," Mason said. "He'll think it over for ten or fifteen minutes, then he'll be afraid not to act. He'll get hold of the authorities here and tell them to pick up Mabel Norge and question her as a material witness."

"And what will we be doing?" Della Street asked.

"We," Mason told her, "will be driving to Los Angeles in order to catch a night plane back to Fresno so we can be on hand in the morning and blow the lid off in case Vandling wants any more action in court."

Chapter 14

By the time court convened at 10:00 A.M. word had passed around that the case of the People of the State of California versus Myrna Davenport was no ordinary preliminary and the courtroom was jammed.

Talbert Vandling grinned at Mason as Mason, accompanied by Paul Drake and Della Street, entered the courtroom.

"Thanks for the tip on Mabel Norge."

"Did you get her?"

"We nailed her."

"What's her story?" Mason asked.

"She hasn't any."

"What do you mean?"

"She came here in company with a San Bernardino deputy sheriff. By the time she arrived here she'd decided she wasn't going to talk. She's retained an attorney here who advises her to keep quiet."

"Serve a subpoena on her?" Mason asked.

"Sure."

"How about Los Angeles?"

Vandling smiled and shook his head. "They're being very, very coy. They want us to dispose of the matter up here."

"What are you going to do?"

"I'm going to go ahead for a while. I can always dismiss. And then, of course, I may have something up my sleeve that I don't care to disclose to you at the moment since we're in adversary positions."

"Why should we be?" Mason asked.

"Because you're attorney for the defense and I'm attorney for the prosecution."

"What do you want to do?"

"I want to convict the murderer of Ed Davenport."

"So do I."

"There may be a difference of opinion. You think your client is innocent."

"Don't you?"

"Hell, no."

Mason said, "Give me a little elbow room and I'll disclose some facts that will startle you."

"You can have all the elbow room you want," Vandling said, "as long as you're disclosing facts."

"Thanks."

"Now wait a minute," Vandling said. "You wouldn't try to be slipping one over on me, would you?"

Mason shook his head. "I'm trying to get Myrna Davenport acquitted but I want to apprehend the murderer of Ed Davenport."

Vandling said, "The district attorney in Los Angeles gave me quite a briefing about you. He told me you were tricky, shrewd, diabolically clever, and while he didn't say in so many words that you were crooked he intimated that you'd cut your grandmother's throat in order to obtain an advantage for a client."

"Why not?" Mason asked, grinning. "After all, I'm supposed to represent my clients. Then again you're not my grandmother."

Vandling said, "If I can convict your client of this murder, Mason, and I think she's guilty, I'm going to do it. If you can get her released you're going to do it. Those things are understood. Otherwise I'm willing to ride along with you."

Mason said, "I'm accepting your assurance that you don't want to convict her unless she's guilty."

"I don't."

"How about riding along and doing some exploring to find out who is guilty?"

"That's okay by me," Vandling said. "I told you I was going to take a chance on you, Mason. I'll co-operate."

"Here we go," Mason said. "Here comes the judge."

Judge Siler entered the courtroom, the bailiff pounded the court to order, the spectators were seated and Mason, leaning across to Vandling, said, "Call Mabel Norge as your next witness. See what she has to say."

"Will she jerk the rug out from under me?"

"The rug's already been jerked out from under you," Mason told him. "You're in the air. It's just a question of what you fall on that's going to count."

"I'd like to fall on my feet," Vandling said.

"Try calling Mabel Norge."

Vandling regarded Mason for a moment, then said, "If the Court please, I want to recall Dr. Renault, but I would like to interrupt his testimony for a moment to call another witness."

"No objection on the part of the defense," Mason said.

Judge Siler merely nodded.

"Call Mabel Norge," Vandling said.

Mabel Norge reluctantly arose, bent over for a few final words with an attorney who was seated next to her, then marched up to the witness stand and was sworn.

"You were employed by Edward Davenport during his lifetime?" Vandling asked.

"Yes, sir."

"When did you see him last?"

"On the eleventh."

"That was Sunday?"

"Yes, sir."

"And where did you see him?"

"In Paradise."

"And after that what happened?"

"Mr. Davenport was driving to Los Angeles. He left Paradise around noon and intended to drive as far as Fresno that evening."

"Did Mr. Davenport leave you any final instructions when he left?"

"I don't know what you mean by final instructions," she said, hurrying her speech as an indication she was trying to get her story in before she was stopped either by Court or counsel. "Mr. Davenport had left me instructions that in the event of his death I was to see that the contents of an envelope were delivered to the authorities. He told me that his wife was trying to poison him and—"

"Just a minute," Judge Siler said.

"Yes," Vandling observed. "What Mr. Davenport may have told you would not be binding on the defendant, unless, of course, the defendant was present at the time."

"We have no objection," Mason said. "Let's get the conversation into the record."

"For what purpose?" Judge Siler said. "It would be hearsay."

"I'm not certain," Mason said, "but that it might come within one of the exceptions to the rule of hearsay evidence. I have no objection."

Judge Siler hesitated.

"Well," Vandling said, "I'll get at it this way, Your Honor. Prior to the last time you saw Mr. Davenport, had he given you an envelope?"

"He had. Yes, sir."

"And what did you do with that envelope?"

"I placed it in a lockbox in my desk."

"And did Mr. Davenport give you any instructions in connection with that envelope?"

"Yes, sir. He said that his wife was trying to poison him and that in the event of his death I was to turn this envelope over to the authorities, that his wife had poisoned her cousin and that—"

"Now certainly," Judge Siler said, "this is hearsay."

"It might be part of the *res gestae*," Mason said.

"*Res gestae* of what?" Judge Siler asked caustically. "This is a most peculiar situation. Counsel for the defendant seems not only willing but anxious to permit the introduction of hearsay evidence damaging to his client, evidence which the Court cannot take into consideration in the case. The Court won't consider any further evidence as to conversations which took place between the witness and the decedent unless it can be shown that it was in the presence of the defendant."

"I'd like to cross-examine on it," Mason said.

Judge Siler shook his head. "The Court is not going to permit the record to be cluttered up with hearsay evidence whether counsel desires it or not. After all, there are certain rules of evidence. The Court thinks that counsel should object to evidence detrimental to his client which is plainly improper as being hearsay.''

''Thank you, Your Honor,'' Mason said.

Vandling glanced at Mason.

Mason grinned back.

''You agreed with Mr. Davenport that you would do certain things in connection with this property upon the happening of certain events?'' Vandling continued.

She hesitated a moment, then said, ''I don't think I have to answer that question.''

''Why not?''

An attorney arose from the back of the courtroom. ''If the Court please,'' he said, ''I am representing Miss Norge. I am willing to state certain matters to assist in helping clear up a murder case. I am willing to suggest ideas which we may treat as potential facts, but which my client will not admit under oath.

''I suggest that it *may* be a fact that Miss Norge, a loyal, competent secretary, was given instructions to do certain things, thinking that by so doing she was helping consummate a mining deal which was of the greatest importance to Edward Davenport.

''That upon learning of the death of her employer she tried to carry out the last instructions he had given her, but later, having communicated with the district attorney of the county in which she resided, she was advised that under the law all property belonging to the Davenport estate must be impounded for probate.

''Since she felt the widow, who is the defendant in this action, was hostile to her employer's interests and had poisoned him—please understand I am only relating her sincere feelings which are not evidence in this case—her attitude toward the widow and the widow's attorneys was noncooperative.

''Technically some of the things she might have done might have been contrary to statute. I therefore advise her not to answer that question.''

Vandling pursed his lips. "On Monday, the twelfth, you went to the bank at Paradise and made some deposits?"

"I did."

"And some withdrawals?"

"I did."

"The withdrawals were in the form of cash?"

"They were."

"And where is that cash now?"

"My attorney has placed it in a safe-deposit box."

"Do you claim that cash?"

"I certainly do not."

"Who owns that?"

"It is a part of Mr. Davenport's estate. I may state that each deposit that I made and each withdrawal that I made was in accordance with his specific instructions."

Vandling glanced at Mason.

Mason shook his head.

"That's all," Vandling said. "Any cross-examination?"

"Yes," Mason said. "You have said that everything you did was under instructions given you by Mr. Davenport."

"That is right."

"And didn't Mr. Davenport advise you to take this cash to San Bernardino?"

"Yes."

"And to await instructions at the Antlers Hotel there?"

"Yes."

"And to register under the name of Mabel Davenport?"

"Yes."

"And didn't he advise you that you were to turn this cash over to a certain party no matter what might happen or who might try to stop you or on what ground?"

Mabel Norge's attorney arose and said, "There again I am forced to advise my client not to answer the question. I will say to the Court and counsel that Mr. Mason's surmise may well represent a true statement of fact, but I refuse to permit my client to place herself in the position of admitting certain acts or conceding certain facts."

"That's all," Mason said, smiling.

Vandling looked puzzled.

Mason shook his head and said, "I would like to have Dr. Renault recalled for further cross-examination."

"Take the stand, Dr. Renault," Judge Siler said.

Mason slowly got up from behind the counsel table, walked over to the witness chair and stood looking down at Dr. Renault.

"Doctor," he said, "you saw Edward Davenport as a patient on the morning of Monday, the twelfth?"

"I have already stated that several times."

"And treated him as a patient?"

"Yes, sir."

"And he recited symptoms of arsenic poisoning?"

"Yes, sir."

"You didn't personally see those symptoms?"

"I saw secondary symptoms which could have been identified with the prior initial symptoms which he described. I didn't see the primary symptoms which he had described which had taken place in my absence."

"Very neatly answered, Doctor," Mason said. "Now let me ask you a question which may cause you a little trouble. Did you also see Edward Davenport on the day preceding—on Sunday, the eleventh?"

Dr. Renault said, "That is beside the question. That doesn't have any bearing on my professional treatment."

"Oh yes it does," Mason said. "You saw Edward Davenport when he was registered at the Welchburg Motel here in Fresno under the name of Frank L. Stanton, didn't you, Doctor?"

"I—do I have to answer that, Your Honor?" Dr. Renault asked.

Vandling, suddenly on his feet, said, "You certainly do."

"I'm asking the Court," Dr. Renault said.

"It is a pertinent question. Answer it," Judge Siler said.

"I—yes, I saw him."

"And discussed certain matters with him?"

"I talked with him."

"And you discussed with him certain treatment that you were to give him the next day, Monday, the twelfth, did you not?"

"I refuse to recount any conversation which took place between my patient and me."

"Why?"

"It's a privileged communication."

"Only to the extent that you had to find out necessary symptoms for the purpose of administering treatment."

"My conversation with Mr. Davenport had to do with certain symptoms."

"Mr. Davenport told you that he wanted to die, didn't he?"

"I am not going to mention the conversation I had with Mr. Davenport."

"Mr. Davenport paid you money in order to set the stage so that apparently he could pass away. It was agreed that he was to call you for treatment the next morning and relate symptoms of arsenic poisoning, that you were to help him simulate a state of collapse following arsenic poisoning so that he could apparently pass away while his wife was present. Isn't that true?"

"I'm not going to answer that question."

"You have to answer it," Mason said. "It doesn't relate to any confidential communication."

Vandling, on his feet, said, "If that question is answered in the affirmative it indicates a conspiracy, a crime. It is not a privileged communication, Your Honor."

"It certainly does not call for a privileged communication," Judge Siler said.

"Then I don't have to answer," Dr. Renault said, "because it would incriminate me."

"Do you refuse to answer on that ground?" Judge Siler asked.

"I do."

"This is a most unusual situation," said the judge.

Mason said, "In accordance with this plan which had been worked out and which you and Davenport had carefully rehearsed, you reported that the man was dead. You reported that you would have to call the authorities. You locked up the cabin but didn't call the authorities immediately, giving Ed Davenport an opportunity to get out of the window and jump in a car which had been conveniently parked immediately adjacent to the window of the cabin in which he was supposed to have died, and drive to a predetermined rendezvous. There was a house trailer parked at this place. Ed Davenport had the key to that house trailer. It was equipped with new clothing so that he could get rid of his pajamas and dress himself, wasn't it?''

"I refuse to answer."

"And," Mason went on, "he told you that he had been embezzling money from his wife's separate property, didn't he? And he said his wife had an officious relative who was constantly insisting that Mrs. Davenport demand an accounting and that the game was about up, that he had juggled many thousands of dollars so that he had them in the form of cash, that if he didn't disappear he would be detected and prosecuted. Didn't he tell you that and ask you to help him?''

"I refuse to answer on my constitutional rights."

"And didn't he tell you that he had poisoned Hortense Paxton, that the authorities now suspected that her death had been murder and that he felt they would exhume the body, that he wanted to have them think he was dead when that happened and that you were to be paid generously to help him?''

"I refuse to answer."

"And," Mason went on, "after Davenport went to that house trailer you gave him some whisky containing cyanide of potassium. You knew that he had suitcases containing a large amount of money which he had been accumulating by a process of juggling the assets of his wife. You gave him that whisky and—''

"I did not. I absolutely did not," Dr. Renault shouted. "I had no idea what the suitcases contained. And if you're so smart you had better get the other party to the conspiracy, the one who was going to drive the house trailer over to Nevada for him.''

"You are referring now, I take it, to Jason L. Beckemeyer, a private detective at Bakersfield?''

"I am," Dr. Renault snapped.

Mason turned to Vandling and said, "And now, Mr. District Attorney, I suggest by mutual consent we continue this case, that Dr. Renault be taken into custody and that a warrant be issued for the arrest of Jason L. Beckemeyer. I think that by the time we get done taking a statement from Dr. Renault we'll find out what actually happened.''

Vandling was on his feet. ''The prosecution wishes to announce its indebtedness to Mr. Perry Mason for his excellent co-operation, and at this time, if the Court please, I move to dismiss the case against the defendant, Myrna Davenport.''

Chapter 15

Mason, Della Street, Paul Drake and Talbert Vandling, seated around a table in the living room of Mason's suite at the Californian Hotel, touched glasses.

"Here's to crime," Vandling said.

They drank.

"What gets me," Vandling went on, "is the manner in which the Los Angeles district attorney warned me that you had cloven feet, horns on your head, a tail, and a smell of sulphurous brimstone about you. Thanks to your co-operation with me, people are talking up and down the street about *my* detective ability."

"That's fine," Mason said. "If a few more of them would co-operate with me we might get along a lot better. Tell us about Dr. Renault."

"Dr. Renault made a complete statement," Vandling said. "He was given no promises of immunity or otherwise. After thinking things over he decided he had better clear his conscience as best he could.

"There seems to be no doubt about what happened. You called the turn. Davenport had poisoned Hortense Paxton so his wife would get the Delano money. Then he started turning everything he could get hold of into cash, juggling funds and leaving accounts in a mess. Also he started laying the foundations for his wife's conviction of Hortense Paxton's death if there should be any investigation."

Mason nodded.

"Davenport knew that he might come under suspicion unless he could divert suspicion to someone else," Vandling went on. "So he was very careful to tell his wife, in the presence of Sara Ansel, that he had left a letter with his secretary which was to be delivered to the police in the event of his death, that in that letter he accused her of poisoning Hortense Paxton and of poisoning him because he had become suspicious.

"Apparently that envelope never did contain anything except sheets of blank paper, but he felt certain that his wife, under the aggressive guidance of Sara Ansel, would take steps to see that this envelope was removed if Ed Davenport should die under circumstances that suggested poisoning.

"By planting the impression in the mind of his secretary that his wife really intended to poison him and had poisoned Hortense Paxton, Davenport had the stage all set. He filled two suitcases with cash and started for Fresno in order to arrange his 'death.'

"He had previously made arrangements with Dr. Renault, a physician with a shady reputation, to see that the circumstances of his death were duly carried out in such a way that it would appear he had been poisoned and then someone had whisked his corpse away so that no autopsy could be performed on it.

"Davenport told Dr. Renault it would arouse suspicions if any of his things were missing, so he had purchased a little traveling bag into which he had transferred his toilet articles and the telltale box of candy he had been so careful to obtain—candy which he knew his wife had touched.

"So Dr. Renault with a hypodermic syringe injected poison into every piece of candy, then sealed the holes with a hot needle. Davenport instructed him to use both arsenic and cyanide because he knew the authorities could prove his wife had both poisons.

"Davenport locked his two suitcases full of money in the trunk of the getaway car, and Dr. Renault gave him a physic and an emetic in order to simulate the symptoms of collapse and arsenic poisoning.

"Davenport had arranged things so that he could slip out through the window of the cabin, get in the car which had been left there and drive out two or three miles to a place where a house trailer had been placed all in readiness for his arrival.

"Naturally Davenport wanted to get all of the money out

of the Paradise account. There were some remittances which he expected to arrive on Friday, or by Saturday at the latest. They didn't come in and he knew they wouldn't be in until Monday. In the meantime everything had been arranged for his synthetic death to take place on Monday afternoon.

"Davenport had a tip that they were going to exhume Hortense Paxton's body and he knew that he couldn't wait. Therefore the thing to do was to work out some scheme by which he could loot the Paradise account after his supposed death.

"Mabel Norge was a credulous young woman who had extreme loyalty to him and he had gradually been building up in her mind the idea that his wife had tried to poison him.

"So Davenport told Mabel Norge that he was going home, that he didn't know at what time his wife might try to poison him. He made her promise that she would withdraw every cent from the Paradise bank and that no matter what happened she would take it to San Bernardino, that she was to meet someone at San Bernardino who was working on a mining deal with Davenport. That person was to have a password that would enable her to identify him and then she would turn over the money.

"This man was Beckemeyer, the third party to the conspiracy. Beckemeyer and Davenport had pulled several sharp deals together. Davenport had used Beckemeyer as the dummy through whom he had siphoned cash out of the various accounts.

"When Davenport suggested he might be getting into a jam which would force him to skip the country, Beckemeyer mentioned that he had a doctor in Crampton who would do anything for cash and who was very hard up.

"So Beckemeyer introduced Davenport to Dr. Renault and the scheme was hatched by which Ed Davenport was apparently to die under such circumstances he would be considered a victim rather than a suspect.

"Dr. Renault got five thousand in cash. He says he has no idea what Beckemeyer was to get, probably a lot more than that.

"Beckemeyer was to drive the house trailer to Nevada

while Ed Davenport lay safely in bed in the trailer. In that way even if anyone saw Davenport getting out of the window and started a search, Davenport would be out of sight.

"Beckemeyer was also to provide the getaway car and attend to the details. Dr. Renault was simply to bring about Davenport's simulated death.

"Mabel Norge had been instructed to go to the office in Paradise Monday evening. She was to receive a telephone message as to where to go in San Bernardino, taking the money with her. All she knew was that she might be juggling funds so that Mrs. Davenport couldn't get wind of a deal Davenport was making.

"Now, according to Dr. Renault's story, Beckemeyer must have done some fast thinking. He knew that Davenport was going to have more than two hundred thousand dollars in cash.

"So Beckemeyer conceived a brilliant idea. Why not see that Davenport *really* disappeared. Since this was what Davenport was intending to do, Dr. Renault wouldn't suspect anything because he knew that was exactly the deal Renault was to help engineer.

"The idea, of course, was that it would appear Myrna Davenport had poisoned her husband, that she had first given him poison in the candy, that then she had finished the job when she was left alone with her husband who was then supposed to be in a dying condition. Naturally the conspirators wouldn't have any corpse, so they had to have it appear that Myrna had some male accomplice who had whisked the body out of the window so it couldn't be autopsied.

"Beckemeyer studied the full possibilities of this situation. Sometime before Friday he went out to a place near where the house trailer had been planted and dug a convenient grave. When Davenport, in pursuance of the conspiracy, slipped out to the trailer, Beckemeyer gave him a few drinks and cooked him a meal of bacon and eggs. Dr. Renault said he warned Davenport to get some food in his stomach the very first thing, otherwise he might really collapse.

"Davenport ate the bacon and eggs and then he and Beckemeyer had a few more drinks, toasting the success of the conspiracy. Beckemeyer slipped a slug of cyanide of potassium in Davenport's whisky. Davenport died almost instantly. Beckemeyer took him out and planted him in the grave, then drove away with the house trailer.

"But Beckemeyer knew there was about thirty thousand dollars in the Paradise account that was to be reduced to cash. He had been instructed to give Mabel Norge the message as to where to take this money in San Bernardino. It was planned that Beckemeyer would call the Paradise number, phone just the address and hang up fast before the call could be traced in case of any hitch in the Paradise scheme.

"Beckemeyer was smart. After he got crossed up on the delivery of the money in San Bernardino he realized that he might have put himself in a vulnerable position, that he might have been talking with someone other than Mabel Norge when he called the Paradise number. So he immediately adopted the position that Davenport had retained him as a private detective to go to San Bernardino and watch the motel unit in question and wrote you a letter that would account for his trip to San Bernardino.

"Now that's generally Dr. Renault's story. It's probably true. Beckemeyer, however, will probably try to blame the murder on Dr. Renault. By the time we get done we'll have each of them singing like canaries."

"Why was Dr. Renault so stubborn about that cyanide?" Mason asked.

"Dr. Renault said he knew what must have happened just as soon as he learned about the cyanide at the autopsy. He was preparing his own defense even then. If he had ever admitted that there had been even a single symptom of cyanide poisoning while *he* was treating Ed Davenport, he would have crucified himself in case the true story ever came out.

"If it hadn't been for the children finding that grave, we would never have known what happened. A convincing case of poisoning would have been made out against Myrna Davenport. She probably would have been convicted."

Mason chuckled. "You can imagine how Dr. Renault felt

when the body was found and the autopsy showed poisoning by cyanide."

"Well," Vandling said, "thanks to your co-operation I've had a nice feather in my cap. People here are patting me on the back and they're going to keep patting me on the back. The thing that I can't understand is how the devil you figured it out."

"I didn't figure it *all* out," Mason said, "but I knew that Edward Davenport was the only person who could have been sure he would be taken sick at Crampton. If Davenport had planned it that way, then it was almost certain that Dr. Renault was in on it. And because the grave had been dug it was almost certain that someone else knew it had been planned in advance that Davenport was to be taken ill at Crampton.

"When you come right down to it, Vandling, you have to bear in mind that while Beckemeyer and Renault may have committed the actual murder the one who really put his neck in the noose was Ed Davenport."

"Contributory negligence," Vandling said, grinning.

"Exactly," Mason observed, filling the glasses once more. "Well," he said, "here's to crime."

About the Author

Erle Stanley Gardner is the king of American mystery fiction. A criminal lawyer, he filled his mystery masterpieces with intricate, fascinating, ever-twisting plots. Challenging, clever, and full of surprises, these are whodunits in the best tradition. During his lifetime, Erle Stanley Gardner wrote 146 books, 85 of which feature Perry Mason.